Danger at the Prehistoric House of Horrors!

Just before the evil dinosaur could take a bite out of the New Kids, their cars jerked sideways and they slid into a tunnel where everything went black. The tunnel twisted right, then left. The cars turned upside down again and again. A chill of cold air blasted overhead. Vicious creatures appeared out of nowhere. The New Kids laughed and shouted, enjoying every minute of it.

All of a sudden, the cars spun around and separated from one another. They shot down five different tracks, racing toward unknown destinations, the darkness echoing with the shrieks and cries of long-dead animals . . .

And somewhere in the darkness, the fifth car jerked to a halt. A thick woolen blanket was thrown over the car, and its passenger was instantly tied up with rope.

Suddenly an eerie silence hung in the air. No one moved, no one uttered a sound.

One of the New Kids had been kidnapped!

The Novels

NEW KIDS ON THE BLOCK

Backstage Surprise

Seth McEvoy and Laure Smith

AN ARCHWAY PAPERBACK
Published by POCKET BOOKS
New York   London   Toronto   Sydney   Tokyo   Singapore

AN ARCHWAY PAPERBACK *Original*

An Archway Paperback published by
POCKET BOOKS, a division of Simon & Schuster Inc.
1230 Avenue of the Americas, New York, NY 10020

Text and cover art copyright © 1990 by Big Step Productions, Inc.
Packaged by March Tenth, Inc.

ISBN: 0-671-73170-X

First Archway Paperback printing November 1990

10 9 8 7 6 5 4 3 2 1

Backstage Surprise

Chapter

1

IT WAS PITCH-DARK outside as the New Kids' concert bus moved swiftly down the highway. The bus driver drove all night while everyone else was sound asleep in their bunks.

Joe was the first to open his eyes when the morning sunlight finally streamed through the window. "Where are we?" he asked, waking the others.

Donnie hopped down from his bunk overhead. "Where do you think? We're on the bus. Does this look like your bedroom back home in Boston?"

"No way," said Jonathan. "I've seen his room! It looks like ten thousand screaming fans went in there and tore it apart. It's a mess!"

"It looked more like fifty thousand fans to me," Danny added.

"My bedroom's not a mess," Joe protested. "It's just *creatively* organized."

Danny laughed, but Jonathan's brother Jordan just pulled the covers over his head. Donnie yanked them off. "Wake up. It's six o'clock in the morning. Time to get rocking and rolling."

Jordan groaned. "I'd rather be sleeping and snoring. Last night's concert ran late. We were up until two o'clock in the morning. Can't we stay in bed an extra hour?"

"No way," said Donnie. "There isn't any more food around here. Let's get dressed so we can go have breakfast. I'm so hungry I could eat just about anything."

"Oh, so it was you that chewed a hole in my favorite black shoes," said Jonathan. "I thought it was Nikko."

"When is that dog of yours coming back from the vet?" asked Joe. "I miss having him slobber all over my face in the middle of the night."

"He should be here in a couple of days," Jonathan replied. "The veterinarian told me that his ear infection will be cleared up by then."

Donnie put on one of his trademark peace-sign medallions. He then started digging through the pile of clothes at the foot of his bed, scattering them everywhere. Shoes tumbled on the floor, shirts fell against the window shades, and a brown leather jacket landed on Danny's head.

Danny tossed the jacket back. "What are you looking for?"

"A bag of Oreos. I know they're in here somewhere!"

"If you keep filling yourself with junk food," said Danny, "they're going to declare your body a landfill."

"At least what I eat tastes good. That stuff you buy at the health-food store looks like sawdust and tastes even worse!"

"That's what keeps me strong," he said as he flexed both arms, his muscles bulging.

"Well, if it isn't Danny Schwarzenegger," joked Donnie. "He sings, he dances, he's strong enough to bench-press the Empire State Building!"

Danny threw his hat at Donnie and they

both burst out laughing. The two of them always acted this way, ever since they were in elementary school together. They teased each other all the time, but they were the best of friends, as close as brothers. Almost as close as Jonathan and Jordan. And Joe had become everyone's little brother, just like he was in his own family.

All five of the New Kids on the Block came from big families with lots of sisters and brothers. That experience had helped them learn to get along with different kinds of people, especially one another. Sometimes they had their fights and disagreements, but everyone always made up afterward.

When the bus came to a stop, Joe jumped up and looked out the window. He couldn't see anything. The bus had parked beside a huge brick wall. "Where are we?"

Jonathan pulled on his oversize T-shirt. "Joe, didn't you read the itinerary sheet?"

Jordan finally sat up on the edge of his bunk. "Are you sure our little Joe can read it?" he said playfully. "Joe still needs a tutor until he graduates from high school. Maybe Einstein hasn't finished teaching him his alphabet!" A mischievous smile spread across his face, just as it always did when he teased Joe about being the youngest New Kid. Jordan really liked Joe, but he loved to poke fun at him every chance he could.

"Lay off," said Joe, throwing a pillow at him. "Just 'cause I'm a few years younger than you doesn't mean I'm a little kid who can't even read."

"Chill out, man, I was only kidding."

"I know," he said apologetically. "I'm just tired this morning." He sat down and pulled on his favorite old pair of faded blue jeans. "Does anybody have today's itinerary sheet? I can't find mine."

Jonathan handed him his copy. He always kept his things neatly organized, so he knew where everything was at all times. This was a big help to their manager, Dick Scott. Jonathan had great respect for Dick. He often said he'd like to follow in his footsteps someday.

Joe's blue eyes lit up as he read through the day's activities. "It says here that we're at the Earth Adventure theme park."

"Earth Adventure? What's that?" asked Danny. "I've never heard of it."

"That's because it's brand-new," Jonathan explained. "It's supposed to be the biggest amusement park in the country. It has six roller coasters and millions of other rides.

Each one represents a different country from around the world. We're headlining at tonight's grand opening ceremonies."

"I can't wait to see it," said Jordan. "I love amusement parks."

"Me, too," added Donnie.

"Hey, everybody!" yelled Joe. "It also says that the park is serving us an international breakfast that includes Belgian waffles, Polish sausage, English scones, Canadian bacon, and *Heu . . . v . . . o Ranch . . . er . . . os?*"

"That's a Mexican-type omelet," explained Jordan. "I love 'em."

"This meal sounds like heaven on earth," said Donnie.

"Yeah, a real *earth adventure,*" Danny replied.

Jordan rolled his eyes as he braided his ponytail. He then let out a groan, pretending to be in pain. "Oh, no! I can't take your bad jokes on an empty stomach."

"Well, then, let's break and go do some serious eating," said Donnie, leading the way to the door of the bus.

Just outside, the park officials were lined up and waiting to greet the New Kids, their manager, and all the men and women of the road crew.

"Welcome to Earth Adventure," said a tall thin man in a dark blue suit. "I'm Bill Kane, the park manager."

Dick Scott shook his hand firmly. Dick was a big, strong black man with nerves of steel. He could handle just about anything. And he often had to when he was on tour with the New Kids.

"We're glad to be here," said Dick. "Everyone is looking forward to the concert tonight."

"I'm sure it will be something special," Mr. Kane replied. "The tickets sold out in less than an hour."

Dick smiled proudly. He had worked long and hard handling schedules, travel arrangements, security problems, press interviews, and anything else that came up. He was the one everyone counted on, and he always got the job done.

Donnie stepped forward and introduced the rest of the group to Mr. Kane. "We're the New Kids on the Block. My name is Donnie Wahlberg."

Danny reached out and vigorously pumped Mr. Kane's hand. "Danny Wood, here."

"I'm Jonathan Knight," Jon said in his shy, quiet way.

Jordan, always one to be creative, spun around and did two quick dance steps. "Jordan Knight, at your service."

"Joe McIntyre's my name. Pleased to meet you."

Mr. Kane grinned from ear to ear. He then introduced the group to the other park officials: the assistant park manager, the concert manager, and the head of park security. "Anything you need, these gentlemen are here to provide it for you."

"Anything?" asked Joe.

"What *would* you like, Mr. McIntyre?" inquired the concert manager.

"Do you have a gym or a health club? I'd like to work out later."

"Aren't our concerts enough of a workout for you?" asked Donnie.

"He's trying to impress that girl he met last night," said Jordan.

Joe made a face at him. "I just want to start getting in shape."

"Like me," bragged Danny.

Joe gave him a shove.

"There's a health club in nearby Clarksville," said the concert manager. "We could take you there after you eat and you could have your private tour of the park this morning. Just come by my office anytime before we open at twelve o'clock, and I'll make all the arrangements for you."

Joe gave him the thumbs-up sign. "That'll be great!"

"If you'll follow me," said Mr. Kane, "we have a special breakfast all ready for you."

"Let's go!" declared Donnie.

The main cafeteria was full of park employees dressed in costumes from around the world. They all started buzzing with excitement as the New Kids entered the room and headed for their table.

Mr. Kane gave a short enthusiastic speech, welcoming everyone to opening day. When he was finished, large trays of food were brought in, and he sat down to eat next to Dick Scott.

"Belgian waffles!" exclaimed Donnie. "Now this is what I call a world-class breakfast." He loaded his plate with four waffles. He then topped them with dozens of strawberries and a heaping pile of white powdered sugar.

Danny shook his head. "You've put enough sugar on there to make a hundred dentists wealthy."

"Not me! Didn't you know I brush regularly after every meal? Maybe you should, too, Godzilla-breath!"

"No one has ever complained about my breath."

"Especially not the girls," Joe teased him.

Danny grinned. "That's true." He then turned and asked Mr. Kane about all the rides in the park.

"You'll love the Russian Racers," he began. "We had them specially designed. They're unique gyroscopic unicycles which means, of course, each has only one wheel. You pedal them as fast as you can around a multi-dimensional track."

Danny smiled confidently. His brown eyes sparkled. "That sounds like something I can easily beat Donnie at. I've got stronger legs than he does."

"Just you wait and see," Donnie replied.

"Wait and see what?" asked a young girl, walking up behind them.

Donnie spun around. "What do we have here? One of our fans?"

The thirteen-year-old girl shoved her hands into the pockets of her jeans and looked down nervously. Her long dark hair fell over her face.

"Hey, don't be shy," said Donnie. "We *love* our fans! Without you we'd be back on the streets of Boston breakdancing for spare change."

"This is my daughter, Megan," said Mr. Kane. "I've made arrangements to have her show you through the park this morning."

Jonathan reached over and shook Megan's hand. "Glad to meet you, Megan."

"Same here," said Joe. "Why don't you take a seat?"

Megan grabbed a chair and scooted in between Danny and Joe. She was so excited she could barely breathe.

Dick Scott and the road crew quickly finished eating and were ready to get to work. Dick told the New Kids that, because the park had its own security force, he had given their bodyguards the morning off. He was half-serious when he jokingly pleaded with them to stay out of trouble. Just before he turned to leave, he reminded the group to be at the concert hall by noon.

When Dick left, Jordan pushed his empty plate aside and leaned back. "I can't wait to try out those new rides."

"We don't get a chance to go to amusement parks much anymore," Jonathan said to Mr.

Kane. "Every time we go, we're mobbed by fans. It'll be great to have some fun before the park opens to the public."

Joe winked at Megan. "Don't get the wrong idea. We *love* our fans, but too many of them can be a little crazy."

Danny nudged her. "Of course, Joe's idea of too many fans is a hundred thousand or more. By the way, who's *your* favorite New Kid?"

Megan's face blushed bright red. "Oh, uh, you're all so great—how could I pick only one?"

"Really, we're just ordinary guys," said Danny. "We do regular things like everybody else. Except for Donnie, that is. Look at him! He's eaten so much this morning I think he's going to single-handedly cause farm prices to rise all over the world. How many plates of food have you had, Donnie?"

After gulping the last drop of his papaya juice, he answered, "I'm not counting. I'm just eating a normal breakfast, really!"

"Normal for the New England Patriots, maybe," replied Jonathan. "But *I've* been counting and you've chowed down at least four platefuls."

"No way, it can't be more than three."

Jonathan disagreed. "Three was ten minutes ago."

"And he's still going strong," said Danny. "Donnie the wonder eater! Maybe we could put him on display in the park. Come one, come all! See the fifth wonder of the New Kids!"

Mr. Kane smiled. "Well, I have to be getting back to my office. My daughter Megan will take you on all the rides. She knows every inch of this place better than I do. Our security guards have been instructed to help you any way they can. Each one is dressed in a different costume, but you'll be able to recognize them by their bright red name tags. So I hope you enjoy yourselves, and I'll see you later."

When he left, Danny grilled Megan with more questions about the park.

"Oh, you'll love the Prehistoric House of Horrors," she told him. "The dinosaurs look so real."

"Does it have Mrs. McCreedy in it?" asked Donnie.

"Who's she?"

Donnie smiled mischievously. "She's Danny's first love."

"No way," Danny protested. "Mrs. McCree-

13

dy was our elementary school math teacher," he explained. "She had a mean, angry temper like a vicious *stegosaurus!*"

"Yeah, prehistoric!" said Donnie. He shivered at the thought.

Megan looked at her watch. "We'd better get going. According to the plan—"

"What plan?" asked Jonathan. "I thought we could do whatever we wanted to this morning."

Megan suddenly became flustered. "Plan? Did I say plan? Of course there's no plan. You can go anywhere in the park. But you've got to see the Prehistoric House of Horrors. That's all I meant. It's the coolest ride. There's hundreds of different dinosaurs and a waterfall and . . ."

". . . and Mrs. McCreedy!" added Donnie.

Jordan made a face. "I didn't like her, either. I think I'll stay away from *that* ride."

"No! No!" cried Megan. "You've got to go! It's the *best* ride in the park."

"Don't worry, Megan," Danny said with a reassuring smile. "We're going to go on every single one."

"As long as we're at the concert hall by twelve o'clock," Jonathan reminded everyone.

"Well, then, let's posse up and get things

moving," said Joe. He jumped out of his chair and was the first one through the door. The others were close behind.

Over at the concert hall, the New Kids' road crew, also known as roadies, was already preparing for the evening's performance. Even though the stage had never been used before, the roadies were confident that everything would be up and running by eight o'clock that night.

Four roadies climbed the narrow metal rigging high above the stage and expertly positioned the spotlights. Down below, three other workers put tape markers on the floor to show where the microphones and speakers would go. Everyone worked quickly but carefully. This crew was the best in the business. They had put on shows all over the world.

One of the roadies was a quiet young sound man named Rabbit. He was tall and slim, with thin, light brown hair that casually fell around his eyes. They called him Rabbit because he could hear things that no one else could hear. Nobody was as good as he was at tuning up the sound system to make the New Kids' music come across just right.

Rabbit was busy checking out the backstage

area when he spotted a piece of paper almost completely hidden behind a curtain on the wall. He picked up the paper and turned it over and over, but he couldn't read what it said. Rabbit didn't know *how* to read.

"Hey, Rabbit!" yelled Phil, one of the lighting men. "What's that?"

"Oh, nothing," Rabbit replied. He immediately crumpled up the paper. He didn't want *anyone* to know he couldn't read. If they found out, he feared he would lose his job. And he loved working for the New Kids more than anything. "It's just a piece of trash," he said to Phil.

Rabbit searched for a garbage can but didn't see one anywhere, so he put the note in his back pocket. "Just a piece of trash," he muttered to himself. "It can't be anything important."

Rabbit went back to work and put the note out of his mind, never suspecting that it said:

KIDNAPPING PLAN

1. Go to Prehistoric House of Horrors ride.

2. Make sure he sits in last car.

3. Throw B6 switch when cars split off in different directions.

4. Tie him up with rope and a blanket.

5. Push him into storage compartment of utility vehicle parked out back.

6. Drive to secret hiding place.

Chapter

2

MEGAN EAGERLY LED the New Kids out into the park. Jordan jumped in the air when he saw all the rides bursting out in every direction, each one bigger and better than the next. A giant Swiss chalet stood beside an Indian teepee, and an English castle towered over a Brazilian rain forest. Across from that was the biggest roller coaster the New Kids had ever seen in their lives.

Jonathan was impressed by how every single thing was from a different country: food from Germany, music from Africa, sculptures from

South America, Korean dancers, Roman soldiers, and animals from around the world.

Danny was amazed that each ride was lit up with thousands of different colored lights, flashing to the beat of its international theme music.

Jordan and Joe both seemed to get lost in the swirl of sounds pouring out of every ride. But Donnie barely noticed anything except the smells of exotic foods that filled the air.

"Hey, I want to go inside that thing," said Joe, running over to a huge model of the Leaning Tower of Pisa.

"What kind of ride is it?" asked Jonathan.

"It's for little kids," Megan explained. "It has a giant twisting slide down the middle. You'll like the Prehistoric House of Horrors much better. Let's go there first."

"Not yet," said Danny. "I want to try out those Russian Racers your father told us about."

"Well . . . ah . . . okay," Megan said reluctantly. "They're over there. She pointed to a huge Russian palace with seven golden domes. Colored lights formed intricate designs up the sides of the towering structure. They blinked on and off to the beat of Russian folk music.

The employees, wearing red-and-white cossack outfits, were busy making last-minute adjustments.

Danny ran ahead and was the first one inside. "I'm diggin' this," he exclaimed when the others caught up to him. A multilayered track filled the palace from floor to ceiling. Blue and yellow lights streamed down on the sleek silver cycles lined up at the starting gate.

"How can they stand up with only one wheel?" asked Donnie.

"It's because they have these gyroscopes inside each one," Megan explained. "They keep the unicycle from falling over no matter how clumsy you are."

"Even as clumsy as Danny?" Joe said with a grin.

"Hey!" Danny replied, spinning around in a quick breakdance step. "I'm not clumsy. I'm Mr. Magic on my feet. Let me at those gyrocycles!"

Megan showed everyone what to do. "These things are completely safe. A computer controls everything. They can't crash or run off the track. Just push this button to start the gyro mechanism," she said. "Then hop on, strap yourself in, and start pedaling!"

"Like this?" asked Danny. He stepped back

and leaped into the air. "All I do is—aaagggh!" He jumped up so high he slid sideways off the seat. He hung upside down, his left leg up in the air.

"Haawh! Haawh!" Jonathan bellowed in his loud, thunderous laugh. "Nice moves. Maybe we should work that trick into our act."

"Very funny," Danny replied. "I'm not giving up yet. Here goes! Ride 'em cowboy!" This time Danny strapped himself in and safely took control of the unicycle. He spun the one-wheeler around in a complete circle like an expert. "Nothing to it!" he said, clapping his hands over his head. "Okay, who's going to race me? First one to the top gets to lead the way onstage tonight!"

"Done!" answered Donnie, as he slapped Danny's open palm. "You got yourself a race!" He climbed onto his vehicle and moved it into position.

Joe held up his fingers like a starter's pistol. "On your mark, get set, *go!*"

Donnie and Danny sped off up the first ramp, pedaling as hard as they could.

"Look at 'em fly!" yelled Jordan. "Who do you think's going to win, Megan?"

"Danny," she answered confidently. "He's the strongest."

21

"They're both doin' great," said Joe. "Danny pulls ahead on the straightaway, but Donnie can really spin around those curves."

"Danny's still going to beat him," she said, her eyes glued to the cycles.

"It must be great to be able to come to a place like this all the time," Joe said to Megan. "You're really lucky."

"I don't think so," she said, sounding a little sad. "You guys go to all kinds of great places. I've never been anywhere."

Jonathan stepped up beside her. "But look at all this stuff from other countries. You get to go around the world in eight hundred ways!"

Joe groaned at Jonathan's joke, but Megan didn't reply, as she watched the gyrocycles climb higher and higher. First Danny was ahead, then Donnie edged past him. Danny retook the lead and Donnie lagged behind. Then all of a sudden, Donnie yelled out, "I won!"

"He was just lucky," Danny shouted down to the others.

"Yeah, lucky I raced against you, Grandpa. Maybe we should get you a wheelchair, since you're too slow to keep up with me."

"I'll show you who's slow. I'll beat you back down to the bottom or I'll . . ."

"You'll what? Give me your new black hat?"

"No way! I'd rather give away my right arm!"

"No thanks, I've got one of my own. Besides, yours is too hairy for me."

They both laughed and took off down the ramp, neck and neck all the way.

Jordan was watching the silver vehicles speed closer when suddenly his eyes lit up. "Those gyro things give me a great idea for a new dance step."

"What is it?" asked Joe. "Are you going to breakdance on top of a unicycle?"

"No! I'm going to move like those gyros do when they twist around on the corners." Jordan spun three times in one direction, then reversed in the other direction, all in a split second.

He showed Joe his new step again, but Megan paid no attention. Her eyes were fixed on Danny and Donnie racing for the finish line. The two were still tied, but in a burst of speed, Donnie pulled ahead and crossed it first.

"Give that man a blue ribbon," yelled Joe.

"They should call me Daredevil Donnie. Who wants to challenge me to a grudge match?"

"Not me," said Jonathan. "Let's try out some more rides."

"How about going to the Prehistoric House of Horrors?" Megan anxiously suggested again.

"Hey! Wait a *minute!*" shouted Joe. "What's that over there?" He pointed out the door to a huge triangular building. Crisscross poles covered the sides, and red smoke poured out of the top. "Is that some kind of space-age volcano?"

"No," said Megan. "That's the Killer Krunch Pyramid. It has a maze of moving walkways inside. If you figure out how to get all the way through the maze, you win a prize!"

"Killer Krunch, here I come!" Joe ran toward the pyramid.

"Guess we'd better follow him," said Jonathan, "or he might take off without us, like he did in Chicago."

"And in Tokyo and London," Jordan added.

Megan frowned. "But next we'll go to the Prehistoric—"

"House of Horrors!" said Donnie, putting his arm around her. "We promise we'll get there."

"Are you making fun of me?"

"Of course not," he said, looking deep into

her eyes. "I'm just teasing. I wouldn't say anything to hurt you."

"I know," she replied, shyly looking down at her feet.

"Hey, where did Joe *go?*" asked Jonathan.

"Here I am!" he yelled from high inside the pyramid. But within seconds he had disappeared again.

"Let's get up to the top of that thing!" cried Donnie.

"You can see the whole park from up there!" said Megan.

Everybody soon piled onto the ride's swift-moving conveyor belts, which led them up and down the maze. One moment they were on the edge of the pyramid looking out, the next they were heading through a dark tunnel full of Egyptian hieroglyphics. They all jumped from belt to belt, trying to catch up to Joe.

"There he goes," said Jordan. "He's almost to the top."

"How can we get all the way up there?" Donnie asked Megan.

"I've never made it that far," she said. "This ride is one of the trickiest ones in the park."

Joe disappeared again and then reappeared a moment later. "I won!" he yelled triumphantly.

The others tried to reach him, but they took a wrong turn and were sent back down an exit slide. Moments later, everyone was reunited at the base of the pyramid.

"Hey, it was dynamite up there!" said Joe. "You guys missed a great view of the whole place."

"What prize did you win?" asked Jonathan.

"Look! I got a free book of food coupons. Here's one for a free piece of authentic Italian pizza. There's one for a German knockwurst. And one for a Belgian chocolate ice cream cone. There must be a dozen different coupons here."

"All right!" Donnie exclaimed. "Maybe I can win it from you on the next ride. How about that one over there, the one that looks like the North Pole?"

"You guys can go there later," said Megan. "But right now you've just *got* to see the Prehistoric—"

"House of Horrors," they all replied in perfect harmony. Then they burst out laughing.

"Follow me," said Megan. She quickly rushed past the Irish ferris wheel, the Moroccan merry-go-round, two more gigantic roller coasters, and the huge Niagara Falls water fountain. She was out of breath when she turned the corner and announced, "Here we are, the Prehistoric House of Horrors."

"Hey, look," said Joe. "All the employees are dressed as cavemen. There's Fred Flintstone."

"No, I'm Barney Rubble," replied the blond young man working the controls.

"Well, then that must be Dino," said Donnie, pointing to the huge green dinosaur that towered overhead.

"It's a *tyrannosaurus rex*," said Megan. She then directed the New Kids to the row of cars lined up underneath it. She asked Jordan to take the first one, then she told Jonathan, Donnie, and Joe to climb into the cars right behind him. When she led Danny to the last car, she told him, "Sit here, because this one's got the best view."

"Where are you going to sit?" he asked.

"Uh, er, I have to . . . ah . . . go see about something. But I'll be right back."

"We'll miss you," said Donnie.

Megan smiled nervously and double-checked all of the safety bars. She then signaled to the attendant to start the ride.

"Mrs. McCreedy, here we come!" yelled Danny, as they moved up into the dinosaur.

With a sudden surge of speed, the cars dove down into a tunnel. It was completely black. They swerved sharply to the left, and an eerie voice echoed through the air: "In darker days at the dawn of time, terror stalked the Earth. This is then, that is now, beware! The dinosaurs are *everywhere!*"

"I'll believe it when I see it," shouted Danny. "I'll bet this ride will be like a movie I once saw. They had little lizards wiggling around in front of a camera, pretending to be huge dinosaurs."

"Are you sure that wasn't one of your home movies?" asked Joe.

Danny reached out, grabbed Joe by the neck and pretended to strangle him. Their laughter was soon drowned out by the pounding music blasting overhead. The cars began to spin, and they plunged straight toward a huge waterfall. They picked up more speed as they drew closer.

"Oh, no, I forgot my umbrella," yelled Jonathan.

But just before they were about to crash into the water, it disappeared!

"What was that?" cried Joe.

"It must have been a giant hologram," answered Jordan, as his car spun to the side.

28

Jonathan pointed up ahead. "Check that out. It's coming right this way and it looks hungry."

"It must be a *Donnie*-saurus!" Danny replied.

The huge creature's jaws burst wide open, swallowing up all five cars at once. As they sped into the darkness, the music pounded louder and louder. The New Kids' hearts beat even faster. Their cars began to spin upside down. Giant holographic images of deadly dinosaurs leaped out at them, their jaws dripping with blood.

"Hey, Danny," yelled Donnie. "Maybe we should put something like this in our next concert."

"Yeah, sure," Danny said sarcastically. "We'll scare all our fans away."

"No, we could project big pictures of all our faces up on the stage."

"Haawh! Haawh!" laughed Jonathan. "Show 'em a big close-up of Danny's face and they'll clear out of the theater in ten seconds."

Another huge dinosaur blasted out in front of them, its huge white fangs only inches from their heads.

"There she is!" yelled Danny. "It's Mrs. McCreedy, our old math teacher."

29

"It *is* her!" cried Donnie. "Those eyes! Those teeth! That temper!"

But just before the evil dinosaur could take a bite out of the New Kids, their cars jerked sideways and they slid into a tunnel where everything went black. The tunnel twisted right, then left. The cars turned upside down again and again. A chill of cold air blasted overhead. Vicious creatures appeared out of nowhere. The New Kids laughed and shouted, enjoying every minute of it.

All of a sudden, the cars spun around and separated from one another. They shot down five different tracks, racing toward unknown destinations, the darkness echoing with the shrieks and cries of long-dead animals.

The first car raced toward the glowing mouth of a fiery volcano, while the car behind it swerved in the opposite direction through a thick jungle of huge ferns and gigantic insects. The third car spun in quick circles, then plunged into a battle between two giant roaring lizards, their silvery scales shimmering in the low light. As the fourth car shot straight down to the floor of a deep, dark cave, thousands of small winged reptiles swarmed in every direction.

And somewhere in the darkness, the fifth car

jerked to a halt. A thick woolen blanket was thrown over the car, and its passenger was instantly tied up with rope.

Suddenly an eerie silence hung in the air. No one moved, no one uttered a sound.

One of the New Kids had been kidnapped!

Chapter

3

JONATHAN WAS LAUGHING out loud when the New Kids' cars raced out of the Prehistoric House of Horrors. "Hey, where's Joe?" he asked as the four cars bumped together and came to a halt at the end of the track.

"Look, his car is missing," said Donnie.

Jordan held up his hand for silence. "Wait! I hear something."

The clicking metal sound grew louder as an empty car rolled out of the doorway and slammed into the other four.

"It's Joe's car!" said Danny.

Donnie ran over and searched every inch of it. "He's gone."

"Is something wrong?" asked the young man at the controls.

"I'm not sure," said Donnie. "Joe was here when we started, but now he's turned into the Invisible Man."

Danny snapped his fingers. "I know what happened."

"What?" asked Jonathan.

"Joe switched seats with me in the middle of the ride," said Danny. "I bet he took off again. He'll probably show up any minute, dressed in one of these caveman costumes."

"Yeah," Jordan agreed. "Just like the time he disappeared in London and reappeared two hours later in a bellboy's uniform."

"Or remember that time he snuck out of the hotel in New York?" said Donnie. "And he came back in one of those horse-drawn carriages from Central Park. I wonder where he went this time?"

"I'll bet he's gone to that gym in Clarksville," said Jonathan. "Remember he asked if he could work out somewhere?"

"That's right," Danny replied. "That's probably where he went. I'm sure he'll be back pretty soon."

"I'll take a look inside just to be sure," said the park employee.

Donnie glanced around. "Where's Megan? I don't see her anywhere."

"Maybe she went off with Joe," suggested Jonathan.

"I doubt it," replied Donnie. "I think she had her eye on Danny!"

Danny grinned proudly. "Well, I guess she likes her guys dark and handsome."

Donnie grabbed him around the neck. "You've got that mixed up, Romeo. Only when it's *dark* are you handsome!"

"There's no one in there," said the young employee, poking his head out of the ride.

"He'll turn up in time for rehearsal," replied Jordan. "He always does. So what do we do next?"

Donnie pointed to a giant roller coaster. The cars were shaped like rocket ships that circled over and under a huge model of the Earth. "How about that ride over there?"

Jordan read the sign. "It's *The Apollo 500, An Earth-Shattering Experience.* That sounds hot! I want to go on that!"

"Fine with me," said Danny. "Last one there is a—"

WHOOSH!

Before he could finish his sentence, the other three were already halfway there.

"Where are you going with that utility cart?" asked the security guard at the side gate of the amusement park. He was dressed as a pirate and had a black patch over his eye. His red badge said TONY.

"I have to get something for my dad before the park opens," Megan explained.

Tony waved her on. "Remember, you can't drive that on the main road."

"I won't," she promised. "I'll just take the back road that runs behind my house." She then raced through the gate. Once she was out of Tony's sight, she stopped and turned around to make sure that the storage trunk of the cart was still safely shut. She listened carefully to see if she could hear any signs of struggle from inside. She was relieved that she didn't hear a sound. "He probably thinks he's still on the ride," she thought to herself.

Megan restarted the vehicle and headed down the road, but instead of turning off at her house, she sped right past it. She drove on until she reached the hill overlooking the park.

When the cart jerked to a halt, she barely noticed the enormous park spread out below.

The glittering mass of brightly lit metal structures seemed only a world away. She jumped out, ran to the back, opened the trunk, and swiftly untied the rope. When she pulled off the blanket, she stepped back and cried, "You're Joe! I thought you were *Danny!*"

"I don't *think* I'm Danny," said Joe, climbing out of the cramped compartment. He inspected his fingers. "These are my hands, all right. But I wouldn't mind having Danny's arms," he said, reaching up and making a muscle. "Maybe someday I will." Joe suddenly stopped joking. "Hey, what am I doing here?"

"I don't know," she replied. "I don't get it at all. Danny was supposed to be in the last car. I strapped him in myself."

"I switched places with him just after the ride started. I wanted to sneak away and go to the health club."

"Oh, what have I done?" cried Megan. "This was really a stupid idea. I can't believe I'd do such a thing. I got so excited when I read that the New Kids were coming. I wanted to go on a picnic with Danny so bad that I didn't think about what I was doing. I just went out of control. Look," she said, opening a picnic basket. "I brought all his favorite health foods:

lentil soup and soyburgers, carrot juice and rice crackers."

Joe made a face. "Yuck! Danny's always trying to get us to eat that awful stuff."

"But it's *good* for you."

"Good and disgusting," said Joe. He then reached over and placed his hand gently on Megan's shoulder. "I'm sure Danny would have liked to go on a picnic with you, but he wouldn't have wanted to be kidnapped."

Megan looked down and started to cry. "I didn't mean any harm. Oh, how could I have been so stupid?"

Joe pulled Megan closer and gave her a hug. "Don't worry, it'll be okay. Sometimes when I get excited about an idea, I jump in without thinking. Like right now. Everyone's probably worried about me, wondering where I disappeared to. I didn't think about that when I decided to switch cars with Danny. I just did it. So don't be too upset about all this. But promise me one thing."

"What's that?"

"Don't do it again!"

"Oh, I won't, I promise. I'll even rip up all my plans." She dug into her pocket. "It's gone!"

"What's gone?"

"My plan! I had it all written down. I was looking at it backstage last night, making sure that every detail would work."

"Maybe you dropped it," suggested Joe.

Megan shrugged her shoulders. "It doesn't matter; my kidnapping days are over anyway."

Joe suddenly noticed black thunderclouds overhead. A breeze began to stir, and the sky was turning dark. "We'd better get back. It looks like it might rain!"

KABOOM! A crash of thunder ripped through the air. "It's going to start pouring any minute," said Joe. "Let's get out of here!"

They hopped into the cart, and Megan sped off down the hill. She drove so fast the little vehicle flew in the air as she hit every pothole. Just as they passed the turnoff to the Kane house, it started to rain.

"I'm getting soaked!" cried Megan.

"Maybe we should stop somewhere until this lets up," said Joe. "What's that little building over there?"

Megan turned the wheel and steered toward it. "That's one of our storage sheds. My dad keeps firewood in there. We can wait inside until it stops raining."

"Great!" said Joe. "I don't want to catch a

cold. Because when I have a cold, I sing like a water buffalo. And I dance like one, too!"

Megan laughed. "Well, I sure wouldn't want that to happen." She pulled up to the small wooden storage building, grabbed the picnic hamper, and dashed inside.

Joe was right behind her. "What's with the basket?"

"In case we're stuck here for a while, we might as well have lunch."

"You mean Danny-type health food? No way! I'd rather tear off my sleeve and have a shirt sandwich."

"It's not so bad," said Megan, opening the lid. She took out a round white rice cake. "Are you sure you don't want some?"

"No thanks," said Joe, looking up at the ceiling. He wiped raindrops off his forehead. "The roof is leaking all over me!"

"Oh, no," Megan replied. "I've really made a mess of things."

"At least it's not a mess we can't straighten out," said Joe, as they quickly scrambled over to a dry corner. "I just hope the rain doesn't last too long or I'll be late for rehearsal."

"I really am sorry about all this," she replied. "I just wanted to be closer to Danny. What's he like? I mean, what's he really like?"

"He's the same as any other guy," said Joe, shrugging his shoulders. "We just happen to sing and dance."

"But that's pretty special."

"Maybe, but underneath all that, we're regular guys from Boston."

"That's what it says in all the fan magazines. But sometimes I wonder how much of what they say is true."

"All the good stuff is true," Joe chuckled. "And all the baloney, like who's going to quit the group, or who's secretly engaged, is completely false."

"But is Danny really everybody's friend, like they say?"

"Danny's a great guy. He's so easy to talk to and a lot of fun to hang out with. He always works really hard to get things just right. Donnie calls him a perfectionist." Joe suddenly snapped his fingers. "I've got an idea. When we get back, I'll talk to Danny and arrange it so you two can spend some time together."

Megan's face lit up. "Oh, Joe! Would you? You're almost as wonderful as Danny!"

"Thanks, Megan. That's quite a compliment, coming from you. Maybe I'll try one of your rice cakes after all."

"Great!" She eagerly handed him one.

Joe sniffed it. "Do humans really eat this stuff?"

"Sure! I love them. They taste sort of like popcorn. Ever since I read that Danny eats health foods, I've tried all kinds of things I never even heard of before."

"Hey, it's stopped raining," said Joe. "Maybe we can get back now." They both peeked outside.

"Look, a rainbow!" Megan said excitedly.

"Make a wish," Joe replied.

"I am, I am!"

"I bet I can guess what you're wishing," he teased her. "Does it begin with the letter D?"

"Danny Wood, what a wonderful name!"

Megan hopped in the cart.

Joe climbed in beside her. "Let's move," he said. "The faster the better!"

Megan raced along the dirt road. The little vehicle bobbed up and down with every bump. Joe held on tight when they swung around the corner.

THUD!

Suddenly, the cart spun out of control and into a ditch.

"Oh, no," cried Megan. "We've got a flat tire!"

"How far is it back to the park?" asked Joe.

"A couple of miles, I think."

Joe jumped out and inspected the damage. "Now I'm going to be late for sure," he grumbled, kicking the tire.

Chapter

4

BACK AT THE concert stage, everything was quiet. Too quiet, thought Rabbit. The truck full of electronic equipment was late, and, without it, the roadies had nothing to do. Most of them just waited, lazing in the sun outside, but Rabbit nervously paced up and down backstage. What if the equipment didn't arrive? he worried. What if it didn't get here in time?

Rabbit knew the answer. There wouldn't be a concert tonight. That would mean thousands of disappointed fans. Rabbit didn't want to let them down, but all he could do was pace back and forth. And worry.

"Rabbit, are you busy?" asked Dick Scott.

"No," he said. "Is there any sign of the truck?"

"It's on its way," Dick replied. "They had engine trouble and stopped to get it repaired. I hope everything's okay. I'm concerned about the musical equipment. What if something was stolen on the way here? We've got new drivers, and they could have made up the story about engine troubles. So I want you to check all the equipment the minute it arrives. If we wait until after the concert, then they could claim somebody took it from backstage."

"I'll know if anything's missing," said Rabbit. "I know every piece of equipment we use."

"That's not good enough," Dick said firmly. "We usually inventory the equipment after every tour. Things have been disappearing lately, and I'm suspicious of these new drivers. I want you to check it out today. Here's the list of what should be on the truck. Be careful with it. It's the only copy I've got. Make sure everything is carefully recorded."

Rabbit panicked because he knew he wouldn't be able to read a single word on the list. His sister had taught him to write his name, but that was all. "Why do we need an inventory right now?" he asked, his hand trembling as he clutched the papers. "Shouldn't we set up as soon as the truck arrives? Otherwise we'll run late."

"There'll be enough time," replied Dick. "Don't you worry."

Rabbit had run out of excuses. "Okay," he said reluctantly.

But as he watched Dick Scott leave, he didn't know what to do. If Dick found out his secret, he was sure he'd be fired.

"Hey, Rabbit!" yelled Phil, carrying lighting cables over his shoulder. "I've got a thermos full of fresh coffee. Want some?"

"Yeah, sure," Rabbit answered. As Phil walked toward him, Rabbit wondered if he should ask Phil to help him do the inventory. Maybe twenty bucks . . . No! Phil might tell someone.

Rabbit was lost in thought. What would he do when the truck arrived? he asked himself. Dick expected him to check off each piece of equipment as it was unloaded. Rabbit wondered if he should just check off *every* item on the list. But what if something *was* missing or stolen? Then he'd be in real trouble.

Phil poured two cups of coffee, then put the thermos down on the workbench.

"What have you got there?" asked Phil.

Rabbit laid the inventory list down and picked up his cup.

"Inventory forms." Rabbit suddenly had an idea! He lowered the coffee cup, then let it slip from his hands. "Drat!" he yelled, spilling it all over the papers.

Phil tried to snatch them out of the way, but it was too late. He then pulled out a handkerchief and tried to wipe up the coffee. "Oh, no! The ink is smearing. Sorry, Rabbit, it looks like I've ruined them."

Rabbit shrugged his shoulders and tried not to let Phil see how relieved he was. "It's okay. It's my fault."

When Phil left to adjust the lights, Rabbit just stared at the coffee-soaked papers. Perspiration beaded up on his forehead. Next time this wouldn't work, he thought. What would he do then? Rabbit nervously shoved his hands in his back pockets. He pulled out the piece of paper he had found on the stage earlier and looked down at it sadly. The blur of letters just stared back at him. He couldn't read a word, so he just wadded it up and threw it in the trash where no one would ever find it.

Danny, Donnie, Jonathan, and Jordan went on ride after ride. They were having a great time. They all loved the high-speed action of the South Pacific Cliff Divers Water Slide and the Australian Outback Alligator races. Danny's favorite was the Italian Demolition Derby Bumper Cars. His miniature Maserati creamed Donnie in his Ferrari in no time at all. Jonathan and Jordan liked the Space Station 2099 Anti-Gravity Chamber the best. Their weightless bodies leaped and danced through the air, spinning upside down, moving to the energetic beat of synthesizer music. And Donnie loved the food—all the food: the egg rolls, the tacos, the calzones, the strudel. He ate everything in sight.

When the four came off of the Turkish Wonder Wheel, a burst of thunder sounded overhead.

"Hey, it's starting to rain," Jonathan said. "Let's go inside before we get drenched."

Jordan pointed to the Chinese Palace of Mirrors. "Why don't we go over there?"

"I'm into it," Donnie replied.

"Not before me, you're not," said Danny, racing ahead. Donnie caught up to him just as they reached the giant red dragon that circled around the iron front gate. The attendant, dressed in a bright blue oriental kimono, admitted the four New Kids into the huge Chinese pagoda. "What you see may be an illusion," she said mysteriously. "Or it may be real." She then shut the massive door behind them.

Inside, every wall was covered with dozens of mirrors, each one a different shape and size. *"Walk into any mirror,"* a deep voice boomed over the loudspeaker. *"Enter the secret world of the hidden and unseen."*

"So here goes," said Donnie, heading for a long narrow pane of glass. He boldly walked up to its smooth, silvery surface and . . . vanished!

"Nice moves," said Jordan. "I wish I had one of these when those girls were chasing me down the streets of St. Louis." He stepped up to a mirror and immediately disappeared inside.

"That's great," Danny said to Jonathan. But Jonathan didn't answer, he just popped through the mirror after Donnie.

"Don't leave me behind," Danny said to an

empty room. He then stepped toward the nearest mirror and—*BUMP!* The glass just shook and shimmered.

"Owww!" Danny yelled, holding his nose. "I thought I could walk through the mirrors!" He tried the next one. It was as solid as a rock. "What's going on?"

As Danny searched for a passageway, Donnie stood alone in a small dark room. He tried to go back through the mirror, but he couldn't. His reflection just stared right back at him. "A minute ago this thing was like water," he muttered. "Now it's like polished steel."

All of a sudden the little room began to glow. It became brighter and brighter until a giant ball of fiery blue light sped straight at Donnie. He ducked. The fireball whizzed over his head. "Some illusion! Hey guys, where are you? Can anybody hear me? Danny? Jordan? Jonathan?"

More fireballs shot at him, faster and faster. The room started to spin. Donnie struggled to keep his balance. The fireballs turned into baseballs that turned into flowers bursting into bloom. Then the huge image of a giant dragon leaped out at him. "Hey, that might be a nice effect for a video," he said.

Jordan had stepped into a dark chamber where the walls began to pulsate with all the colors of the rainbow. The speeding light quickly rose and fell to the rocking beat of the oriental music. As the sounds grew louder, Jordan began dancing across the narrow room, following the rainbow up and down.

While Jordan was mesmerized by the rhythm of the lights, Jonathan was feeling his way along in the dark. The floor began to shift, and without warning, a huge face lunged at him. "Whoa!" he yelled, jumping back. The gigantic twisted head had glowing red eyes. Jonathan thought it looked familiar. It was *his* face!

Jonathan turned and raced to the right. There it was again. His own face, mangled and misshapen. He shivered. "It's just a trick."

"I'm not a trick," replied the giant image. "I'm real."

Jonathan spun around and ran in the opposite direction. But there it was again. "How do I get out of here?" he yelled, as he searched along the panes of glass.

"You're not leaving," said the huge face. "Not yet!"

* * *

Danny was still in the first room, trying to find an opening through the mirrors. One of them had to go somewhere, he thought. He ran his hands across each glass. Suddenly, it went through! He felt a chill of cold air as he spun into the darkness, and then, just as suddenly, he was outside the Chinese Palace of Mirrors. It had stopped raining, and the sun had broken through the clouds. The girl in the blue kimono asked, "What did you think?"

"Not much. I just went in and came right out again."

"You can try it again if you like. Every mirror is different, no visit the same."

All of a sudden Donnie stepped out into the sunlight. "Hi, Danny, any mail for me while I was gone?"

Just then, Jordan popped through another mirror with Jonathan right behind him. "Boy, am I glad to see *your* faces," he said. "That place sure was eerie."

"Was it all an illusion?" asked the attendant. "Or was it real?"

Jonathan shuddered.

Chapter

5

MEGAN HELPED JOE tighten the bolts on the spare tire. "We did it!" she exclaimed.

"That's a relief," said Joe. "If we hurry, I might make it back on time. But *I'm* driving! Okay?"

Megan nodded. "I'll show you how it works."

When Joe pulled the cart up to the side gate, there was a different guard than before. This one was dressed as a Spanish swordsman. "Who's your boyfriend?" he asked Megan.

She turned bright red. "He's not my boyfriend. He's one of the New Kids on the Block."

"Which block?" asked the guard. "I thought you lived out in the country."

"No, that's the name of his rock band," she explained.

"We're playing at the park tonight," Joe added.

"Oh, of course," said the guard. "New Guys from the Block."

"New Kids *on* the Block!" yelled Megan.

The guard laughed and waved them on.

It was almost noon, and the park was about to open. All the rides were ready and waiting; the employees stood out in front in their brightly colored costumes from around the world. A brass band was tuning up as Joe darted around the Tijuana Tumbler, a huge triple-decker ferris wheel.

Joe whizzed past the Peruvian Funhouse and the Niagara Falls Fountain before he pulled up to the huge concert theater where he and the New Kids were to perform that evening. The giant marquee on the side of the white brick building had all their names lit up in red flashing lights. Huge posters hung on both sides of the main entrance.

Joe scowled at his picture when he and Megan ran through the door.

"Hey! There's Danny," said Megan, as they entered the concert hall.

Jordan, Jonathan, Donnie, and Danny sat on the edge of the huge stage, eagerly waiting to get to work.

"Hey, Joe," yelled Donnie. "Where have you been?"

Megan grabbed Joe's arm. "Remember your promise," she whispered.

Joe patted her hand and smiled. "I won't forget."

"What have you been doin'?" yelled Jonathan.

"Did you go to that health club in Clarksville?" asked Jordan.

Joe shook his head. "No, I was just wandering around the park. I hope you guys weren't worried."

Danny laughed. "Worried about you? We didn't even notice you were gone. Now that you mention it, I thought it was a little quiet around here."

Megan shot a glance at Joe. He winked back.

Dick Scott entered the theater. "One, two, three, four, five," he counted out loud. "Well, guys, we've got a big concert tonight; are you ready to rehearse?"

"Always," said Jonathan, jumping to his feet. "Wait till you see the new dance steps Jordan came up with today."

A woman from the road crew ran into the theater and yelled, "Dick, the equipment truck just arrived!"

"Thanks, Janet," he replied. "It's only four hours late! Could you find Rabbit for me and tell him I need to see him?"

"Will everything be ready in time?" asked Jonathan.

"No problem," said Dick. "That is, if one of you doesn't break a leg or disappear somewhere!"

"Who, us?" Donnie asked playfully.

"Yeah, you!" Dick replied, with a twinkle in his eye.

Donnie pretended to look innocent. "You must have us confused with some other New Kids."

Rabbit was nervous as he climbed the steps to the stage. "You wanted to see me, Dick?"

"The equipment truck just came in," he said. "You can get started on the inventory now."

Rabbit stared down at the floor. "Uh, I accidently spilled coffee on it. All the pages are ruined. I'm really sorry."

Dick let out a heavy sigh. "That was the only copy I had."

"I can do the inventory anyway," said Rabbit. "I know what's supposed to be there."

Dick stopped short and thought for a moment. "Well, then I guess that's all we can do. Just be sure to check everything very carefully."

"You got it," Rabbit replied with a nod.

Dick placed his arm on Rabbit's shoulder. "I'm going to round up the rest of the crew. Be sure you're all at the meeting in ten minutes. All except you."

"Me?" asked Rabbit.

"Yeah, I want you to guard the truck while we're gone."

"Sure thing," he answered, relieved that he wasn't in trouble.

When Rabbit and Dick left the stage, Joe yelled to Danny, "I've got a question for you." Joe then went over and whispered in his ear.

Danny nodded, then turned to Megan. "Hey, Megan, let's go for a little walk."

"Okay," she said, grinning from ear to ear.

"Don't forget," said Jonathan. "We've got a meeting to go to."

Megan looked down sadly.

"There's ten minutes before it starts," said Danny. "How about a quick tour of the balcony, Megan?"

"You mean it?" she asked.

"Absolutely," he replied.

Jonathan watched as they headed toward the stairs. "It looks like Megan's got a big crush on Danny."

"Yeah, I guess every girl has her favorite New Kid," replied Joe.

"Are you jealous, Joey Joe?" asked Jordan.

"Who, me?" he answered with a laugh. "I've got enough fans!"

"I'll say," said Donnie. "Sometimes I think you've got more fans than the rest of us."

Joe jumped up on the stage. "They just know when they see the *right stuff!*"

Danny smiled at Megan when he opened the stairway door for her. Megan suddenly became so flustered she stumbled on the first step.

"Are you okay?" he asked, helping her up.

"Oh . . . ah . . . yeah," she awkwardly replied. "I guess I'm kind of nervous."

"I get that way sometimes," he said. "Especially around girls."

"Really?"

"Oh, sure. I always worry I'll say the wrong thing or make a fool out of myself."

"Not you; you could never do that."

"Don't I wish, but I do."

Megan immediately felt better. She never thought that Danny could have the same fears as she had.

When they climbed up to the balcony, they saw the whole theater spread out in front of them. Thousands of red velvet seats circled around the towering stage. Ribbons of dark green carpeting carved narrow pathways through the neat rows, and thin bands of blue lights ran along the edge of the ceiling. "This is one of my favorite sights in the whole world," said Danny. "An empty theater before a concert. There's an energy in the air that makes me want to—"

"Sing and dance?" asked Megan.

"That's right!"

"Well, I can't wait to see that," she added. "I've never been to one of your concerts before."

Danny flipped open one of the red theater seats, and Megan sat down.

"You guys are lucky that you get to travel all around the world," she said.

Danny took the seat beside her. "I can't believe it, either. Sometimes when I wake up, I think I'm back in Boston, getting out of bed for another day at school. Then I'm surprised when I realize I'm in New York, or Paris, or Rome."

"I'd rather go to those places than go to school any day!"

"Hey!" said Danny. "School's the place to be. If it hadn't been for Trotter Elementary, I wouldn't have met Donnie, Jonathan, or Jordan. And there wouldn't be a band. And I wouldn't have met you, either."

Megan was so excited she couldn't say a word. Here she was, all alone with Danny Wood. She just stared into his dark brown eyes. She barely heard him when he asked, "So what's your favorite subject at school?"

"Oh, ah . . . I like art class the best. What was your favorite subject?"

"Mine was English. I had a scholarship to go to Boston University, but my teachers said I should postpone college and tour with the band instead. I'll go back later."

"Boston University," Megan said thoughtfully. "Maybe that's where I'll go to college."

"Boston's a great town," Danny replied.

"There's tons of stuff to do there: You can go to concerts and clubs, ride the subways or the ferry boats, hang out at the parks or the museums. And there's lots of history everywhere.

"Hey, loverboy!" yelled Jonathan from down on the stage. "We gotta go!"

"I'll catch up with you in a minute," Danny shouted back.

"All right," Jonathan answered. "See you there!"

"It must be weird, living with all of them," said Megan.

"The New Kids are like a family," Danny explained. "We really have so much in common that it's always a good time."

"It must be hard to be away from your real family so much," said Megan.

Danny nodded. "Yeah, I miss 'em. But we stay in touch by phone, and every chance we get, we go home for a few days. I sure wish we didn't have to leave here tonight."

"Me, too," Megan said shyly.

Danny glanced at his watch. "I'd better get to that meeting. Dick doesn't like it when we're late."

"Does he yell at you?"

"Dick?" Danny laughed. "No way! He's the best. You can talk to him about anything."

"My dad's the same way," said Megan, standing up to leave. "Danny, you've been really nice to take the time to talk to me."

"Don't thank me, I enjoyed it," he said, reaching out for her hand. Megan's heart nearly skipped a beat as Danny gently folded his fingers around hers and led her to the stairs. When he opened the door, he turned and said, "Hey, I've got a great idea. Why don't you come backstage before the show? You can watch our concert from there." He reached into his pocket and pulled out a yellow plastic backstage pass. "Maybe I can find a tour jacket for you. Would you like that?"

"You bet!" she said, tightly clutching the yellow card. "Do you think I could also watch you rehearse this afternoon?"

Danny shook his head. "It would be okay with me, but some of the other guys wouldn't like it, because we save all our mistakes for rehearsal."

"What mistakes?" asked Megan. "You guys are perfect."

"Thanks," Danny replied. "But we're always trying out new routines in rehearsal, and sometimes we goof up pretty bad. It takes a lot of practice to get it just right. But if we didn't add new things to our act, we'd become the 'Old Kids on the Unemployment Line.'"

Megan smiled, and they silently walked hand in hand down the stairs.

When they reached the stage, Danny stopped suddenly. "Wait! I hear something. It sounds like a fight."

"I think you're right," said Megan, running over to the window. "Look, down there," she cried, pointing outside. "Those two guys are beating up Rabbit. We've got to help him."

But when she turned around, Danny was already gone. He had raced down the stairs.

He flew out the back door just as a man in white coveralls punched Rabbit in the stomach. Rabbit fell to the ground beside the equipment truck. The man then ran to the cab of the truck, and another man, also dressed in white, jumped in the passenger door. "Hit the gas!" one of them yelled.

"Hey, come back here!" shouted Danny, tearing after them.

The truck quickly began to pull away, the back tires spitting out gravel as they picked up speed.

Danny grabbed ahold of the bumper and dived into the truck through the rear door.

"Wait for me!" cried Megan, running as fast as she could.

When the truck started around the corner, it slowed down just enough so Megan could grab Danny's hand and jump inside.

Chapter

6

Rabbit struggled to his feet. His head was whirling as he ran to find Dick Scott. He burst through the door of the meeting room and yelled, "Somebody stole the equipment truck!"

"What happened?" shouted Dick. "Who did it?"

"Two guys in white coveralls. I didn't see their faces. I tried to stop them, but they overpowered me. Then Danny ran after them."

"What do you mean, Danny? Danny Wood?"

"Yeah. When the truck took off, Danny jumped in the back."

Dick shook his head as he paced across the floor. "Why did he do that? He won't be able to stop them. Those guys will overpower him, too. I just hope they don't hurt him."

Jonathan, Jordan, Donnie, and Joe leaped to their feet and were almost to the door when Dick yelled, "Hold it!"

"We've got to find Danny before something happens to him," said Donnie.

"I know how you feel," Dick replied. "But the park just opened to the public, and I want you four to stay right here where you'll be safe from all those screaming fans. I'm as concerned as you are. Once those guys find Danny in their truck, they'll probably take him with them. They can't leave him behind. I'll do everything in my power to see that we catch them."

"I guarantee that the thieves won't get out of the park," said Mr. Kane. "I've alerted every security guard in the place, and they've already sealed off the exits. No one will leave here without a thorough search. I've also contacted the local police, and they should arrive any minute to assist us."

"Good," said Dick. "Our road crew can help, too. Right, gang?"

"Absolutely," replied a short muscular man, standing beside Dick.

"We'll do anything," added one of the women on the lighting crew.

"I knew I could count on you," said Dick. "So, everyone go with Mr. Kane, and he'll show you what to do." When they started to leave, he asked Rabbit and Biscuit, one of the bodyguards, to stay behind.

He then turned to Jonathan, Jordan, Donnie, and Joe. "I know you want to help, but I think you guys should stay here. You'll be mobbed if you go out in the park. And that might make it even harder for us to find Danny."

The four singers reluctantly agreed. They knew what could happen when they showed up: Riots broke out!

"Rabbit, can you remember anything else about the two men?" asked Dick. "Even the smallest detail might give us a clue about who they are or where they went. And are you sure Danny is with them?"

Rabbit nodded his head. "Yeah, when the

truck started moving, Danny raced after it and jumped inside the back end. And that girl ran right behind him."

"What girl?" asked Dick. "You didn't say anything about a girl."

"Uh-oh," said Joe. "I bet it was Megan."

"I don't know her name. But she was hanging around you guys earlier. She was about thirteen or fourteen years old and had long brown hair."

"That's Megan," said Joe. "She'd follow Danny anywhere."

"What were the two men wearing?" asked Dick.

Rabbit tried to think, but his head was pounding. "They had on white coveralls, with red writ—" Rabbit froze. He couldn't tell them what else he knew. He just couldn't.

"Red writing?" asked Donnie. "Was it the name of a company?"

"Come on, Rabbit," said Jordan. "What was written on the coveralls?"

"I . . . I . . ."

Dick sensed something was wrong. "It's okay, Rabbit, just tell us everything. It will be all right."

Rabbit looked down at the floor. He rubbed his feet together as everyone anxiously waited for an answer. He didn't know what to say. But he knew he had to say something—and fast. Danny's life was in danger. He took a deep breath. "O-okay," he stammered. "I got a good look at the writing, but I didn't know how to read what it said."

Dick looked puzzled. "Do you mean it was in a foreign language?"

"No," said Rabbit, shaking his head slowly. "I couldn't read it because . . . I . . . don't know how to read." He let out a deep sigh, half relieved and half afraid of how everyone would react now that his secret was out.

The room fell silent. Everybody was stunned. Dick was the first to speak. "I was beginning to wonder about that. Now a few things make sense."

"Am I fired?"

"We'll talk about it later. Right now I want you to help us find Danny!"

"And Megan," said Joe.

"And all the equipment," added Jordan.

"That's right." Dick nodded in agreement. "Without the keyboards, guitars, amplifiers, and speakers, there won't be a concert to-night."

"Without Danny," said Jonathan, "there won't be a concert *ever!*"

Dick put his hand on Rabbit's shoulder. "Let's you and I go out and cover every inch of this place. You might spot something that will give us a clue." He then turned to Biscuit, the bodyguard, and asked him to stay with the New Kids while he was gone. "You keep a sharp eye on these guys, Biscuit. I don't want them to leave the theater."

"Sure, boss," replied the big muscular black man. "They won't get away from me!" He looked over at Donnie. "Not this time." Donnie and the others were notorious for finding ways around him. But Biscuit was determined not to let it happen again.

Dick quickly grabbed up his briefcase. "I'll let you know the minute I find out anything. If you guys can force yourself, you might do some rehearsing. It would take your mind off all this for a while."

"Fat chance," said Joe.

"Just don't get into trouble," Dick warned, as he and Rabbit headed for the door.

"Do you guys feel like rehearsing?" asked Jordan.

Jonathan shook his head. "I'm too worried."

"We've got to do something!" grumbled Joe.

"If we don't, I may start chewing my nails, just like Jordan does."

Donnie stared out into the empty theater, deep in thought. Suddenly a smile crossed his face. He motioned to Jordan. The two huddled together and whispered.

Seconds later, Jordan went over to Biscuit and asked, "When do we eat?"

"I don't know," he replied. "Lunch was supposed to be at twelve-thirty, but nothing's on schedule now."

"We're getting really hungry," said Jordan. "Won't you let us go out and find something to eat?"

Biscuit scratched his chin. "You know I can't do that."

"If we miss lunch," said Donnie, "we'll feel weak and tired, and we won't be able to rehearse this afternoon."

"Or even perform tonight," added Joe, catching on to the plan.

"I've got it," said Jordan, snapping his fingers. "How about if *you* go get some food for us?"

"Well, maybe that will be all right," he replied. "I can be back in five minutes. But don't you dare leave while I'm gone."

"We won't," said Jordan. "Isn't that right, guys?"

The others nodded. "Sure," said Donnie. "We'll stay right here until you come back with the food."

Biscuit pointed to Donnie. "You keep that promise, or I'll eat all your Nacho Cheese Doritos."

Joe pretended to be horrified. "Oh, no, not that! No one dares to come between Donnie and his junk food! Who knows what could happen?"

"I always keep my promise," Donnie said to Biscuit. "We'll be here until you come back with our lunch."

The bodyguard looked doubtful, but he finally agreed to go.

"Get yourself something to eat, too," yelled Jordan, as Biscuit turned to leave.

As soon as he was out of sight, Joe raced for the back door. "Let's go!"

Donnie grabbed him by the collar. "Hold on!"

"I don't get it," said Jordan. "I thought your plan was to ditch Biscuit and then take off to find Danny."

"I told Biscuit I'd wait until he got back.

And we will. But when he gets here, he won't recognize us. And then we can leave without breaking our promise."

"How?" asked Jonathan.

"Come with me and you shall see," he said. "Backstage is our means of escape."

They quickly followed Donnie to the wardrobe room. It was packed full of hundreds of different costumes. "These are what all the park employees are wearing," he said. "If we each put one on, we can safely go out there and search for Danny. No one will know who we really are. Not even Biscuit."

"Now I get it," said Jonathan. "We disguise ourselves by putting on these costumes, and then we walk right past him when he returns."

"You sure go to a lot of trouble to keep your promise," said Joe.

Donnie dug through the rows of colorful clothes. "Here!" he said with a chuckle. "The perfect costume for Joe: a penguin suit! I think you'll look great in this."

Joe protested, but he put on the big black-and-white suit anyway. "What kind of noise does a penguin make?" he asked.

"I don't know; improvise!" Donnie then threw a grass skirt, a Hawaiian shirt, and a long blond wig to Jonathan.

Jonathan reluctantly picked up the wig.

"Hurry up and put it on!" Donnie insisted. "Biscuit will be back in just a few minutes."

"Okay," Jonathan grumbled. "But don't take any pictures of me in this thing."

"Why not?" asked Jordan. "You'll make a cute hula girl. You can welcome me to Hawaii anytime."

"Very funny," said Jonathan. He rolled up the legs of his jeans and pulled on the long grass skirt.

"Let me see," Donnie said to himself. "What should I wear? How about this, gang?" He held up a thick furry vest and a Viking helmet with horns sticking out of each side.

"Haawh! Haawh!" laughed Jonathan. "You're a crazed Barbarian if ever I met one."

"What about me?" asked Jordan. "What ridiculous disguise are you going to make me wear?"

"That, of course." Donnie pointed to a suit of armor standing against the wall. "You're our *Knight* in shining armor."

"My brother's a Knight, too," said Jordan, as he struggled into the bulky metal suit.

"Yeah," replied Joe. "He's a Knight-mare in that hula girl costume."

Jonathan grabbed Joe by the arm and spun him around in a circle. "*Aloha, aloha,* my little furry friend. Would you like to come to a *luau* . . . as the main course?"

"Awk! Awk!" Joe replied. "Only if you're serving fish. We penguins love fish."

Jonathan stepped in front of the mirror. "I don't think I'm going to fool anybody in this goofball outfit. I look like a mangled dust mop."

"Don't worry," said Donnie. "Just wait and see: You'll fool Biscuit." Donnie then straightened his big helmet and slipped a plastic sword in his belt. "Is everybody ready to go?"

"Almost," said Jonathan. "Maybe if I put on a little of this stage makeup, I might look better."

Jordan laughed as Jonathan smeared on mascara and put huge red circles on his cheeks. "Now you're pure perfection, big brother. Prince Charming had better not be anywhere near here or he'll carry you off in a minute."

Jonathan ignored him and straightened his wig.

When everyone was finally all set to go, they headed out into the concert hall and waited for Biscuit. They didn't wait long. He soon came through the front door, his arms loaded with bags of food.

The New Kids started to walk past him. Joe squawked and poked his long beak at one of the paper bags.

"Get away from those," yelled the bodyguard.

"Awk! Awk!" sounded Joe. "Awk! Awk!"

Jordan pulled him away. "He's starving," he said, his voice muffled by the helmet. "This poor little penguin hasn't eaten all day."

Jonathan and Donnie turned to the side and cautiously edged around them.

"Awk! Awk!" squawked Joe, pecking at the paper again.

"Have you got some fish in there for my penguin friend?" asked Jordan, disguising his voice.

"Get that bird-brain away from my food!"

"Come on, Mr. Penguin," said Jordan.

"Awk! Awk!"

"There sure are a lot of crazy people who work here," Biscuit muttered, as the four singers raced for the door.

Outside, they burst out laughing.

"I thought Biscuit was going to tear your head off, Joe," said Donnie.

"Awk! Awk!" he replied.

"Don't worry, little penguin," Jordan joked. "We'll get you some fish to eat. Just as soon as we find Danny, Megan, and the equipment truck."

"Awk! Awk!"

Chapter

7

THE STOLEN TRUCK filled with equipment raced across the northeast corner of the park. It sped behind the rides toward the maintenance sheds. "I didn't expect them to post a guard during the meeting," said Willy, the driver.

"Can't you go a little faster?" asked Ace.

Willy bolted around the corner, and Ace slammed against the door. "If we go any faster, we'll attract too much attention. Besides, we're almost out of here." The big, stocky man then leaned closer to the steering wheel, his dark, brown eyes peering intently out from beneath his baseball cap.

Ace yanked off his blue wool hat and nervously ran his fingers across his short blond hair. He lit up a cigarette just as Willy drove the truck into a large open garage. Willy jammed on the brakes, and he and Ace hopped out of the cab. They swiftly pulled off their white coveralls. Underneath, they had on green park maintenance uniforms with their names embroidered over the pocket.

Willy let out a sigh of relief. "The hardest part's over."

"But we've still got to get this stuff out of the park."

"Don't worry, I got that covered."

Ace threw open the rear door of the truck. "The sooner we get this stuff unloaded, the sooner— *Hey!* We've got company!"

Danny lunged forward, but before he could get out, Ace slammed the door in his face. Danny pounded against it. "You can't get away with this!"

Willy raced around to the back of the vehicle. "What's going on? Who's in there?"

"There's some guy and a girl in there," said Ace. "They must have jumped inside after we took off. What should we do with them?"

Danny beat on the door even harder. "You idiots picked the wrong truck to steal," he shouted. "This stuff belongs to the New Kids, and every cop in the state will be looking for it."

"No one will find us," Willy responded. "Everybody will be looking for *this* truck. But we'll drive out of here through my secret exit in one of the white Earth Adventure maintenance vans."

"But what about those two in there?" Ace asked Willy. "We're in trouble, now that they've seen us."

"Tie 'em up. Use that rope over there."

When Ace reached down to grab the rope, Danny slammed against the door with all his strength.

It burst wide open.

He leaped on top of Ace, as Megan headed for the garage door. "Run for it, Megan!"

"I can't get it open," she cried, tugging at the handle with all her might.

Willy grabbed ahold of her long hair, and pulled her over to the truck.

"Take your hands off me," she shouted.

Danny pushed Ace out of the way and jumped on top of Willy. "Let go of her, you jerk!"

With a burst of energy, Megan twisted around and punched Willy in the stomach.

He doubled over, and she ran back to the door and frantically yanked apart the lock. "Come on, Danny!"

He ran toward the exit.

But just before he could reach it, Ace threw a rope around him and Danny stumbled to the ground.

"Danny!" screamed Megan. "Are you okay?"

He was too dizzy to answer.

Ace grabbed Megan by the arm and dragged her back toward him. "Quick, tie him up," he yelled to Willy. "I'll keep her under control."

"Ooooh, what hit me?" Danny groaned. But before he could utter another word, Willy quickly wrapped a red bandana across his face and tied his hands behind his back. He then shoved a white handkerchief in Megan's mouth and twisted a rope around her arms, pulling it as tight as he could. "Now let's load the van, Ace. We've got to get out of the park right away. We've wasted enough time already."

"What are we going to do with those two?" he asked, lifting the heavy equipment into the rear door.

"Take 'em out to the country and—" He

paused, looked right at Megan, and grinned. She shuddered. "Take 'em out and leave 'em. When we're far away, we can phone someone to pick 'em up."

Megan's eyes met Danny's. They were both relieved that Willy and Ace weren't going to hurt them.

"That sounds good to me," said Willy. When they loaded as much of the equipment as the van could hold, they shoved Danny and Megan in after it and slammed the door shut.

It was completely dark inside. Danny nudged his face against one of the amplifiers and pulled down the bandana. He then leaned closer to Megan until he was almost touching her.

She could feel his breath against her skin.

"Don't move," he said. "I'm going to pull the gag out of your mouth."

Danny gently bit the edge of the handkerchief. The van jerked forward and his lips brushed against her cheek. For a brief moment, they froze with surprise. Danny then pulled his head back and tugged the handkerchief out.

"Thanks!" Megan said shyly.

Danny tried to reach around to untie her

wrists. But they were both wedged in the van so tight that they couldn't move more than an inch.

In the cab of the van, Ace grumbled to Willy, "Can't you drive any faster?"

"Relax! We're in a different truck now. Nobody's looking for us."

"How can I relax? Now that we've got those two kids to deal with."

"Forget it," said Willy. "By tomorrow we'll be halfway across the country. All we have to do is stay calm and drive to the back of the park. Last night I installed a secret exit in one of the fences. No one knows it's there, and once we get through it, we're home free."

Ace grew more and more nervous, because security guards were all over the place, searching everything. When a guard in a Roman soldier costume ran up to their truck, Ace clenched his teeth so hard, he bit right through his cigarette.

"Hey, Willy," said the guard. "Seen anything?"

"No, Saul, how about you?"

"There's not a sign of that rock band's equipment truck anywhere."

When Saul asked to look in the rear of the van, Ace almost jumped out of the cab.

Willy's mind raced. "Marty's just checked it," he said. "All we've got in back is a couple of air conditioners. I have to take them over to the main office right away."

"Well, then I won't keep you," he said and waved them on.

When Willy pulled away, Ace let out a sigh of relief. "That sure was close," he said, nervously lighting another cigarette.

"There are a couple of park security walkie talkies under the seat," said Willy. "Maybe we'd better turn them on and keep tabs on what's happening out there."

Ace handed Willy one of the miniature radios and he turned on the other one.

"All sectors are sealed," said someone through the tiny speaker. "No one will get out of the park."

"Ha!" Willy exclaimed. "Just you wait and see." He drove the van past a group of security men, dressed as sailors, and waved. "We're almost there. My secret exit is just ahead."

When he came around the corner to the metal chain-link fence that ran across the rear of the park, Willy stopped suddenly. A policeman was standing right where he had cut the links. "Oh, no," he cried. "There's a cop over there."

Ace made a fist. "There's only one of him, and two of us."

"But he's got a gun and we don't!" cried Willy, as he spun the steering wheel as fast as he could. He flew off in the opposite direction.

"Okay, what now?" yelled Ace.

"I'm thinking, I'm thinking!" Willy darted through the rows of storage buildings, weaving wildly back and forth.

"I've got it!" he exclaimed. "I'll hide the truck where no one will find it, then tonight we'll cut through another place in the fence and sneak out of here after the park closes. There's a pair of wire cutters in the glove compartment."

Ace slammed his fist down on the dashboard. "That's a stupid idea! What are we supposed to do until then? Go on all the rides? I say we turn back and make a run for it."

"No!" yelled Willy. "We'll hide the van in the back of the vehicle repair shop. No one will be there. Frank's out sick, and Gordy doesn't come in till five. It's full of vans just like this. Nobody will find it there."

"Then what?" Ace asked angrily.

"We'll hide in the tunnels underneath the park. I worked down there when we were building this place, so I know where we can hide. If we just sit tight underground today, we'll be out of here by tonight!"

Ace shook his head. "You forgot about our two little friends in the back. What do we do about them?"

"Take 'em with us into the tunnels!" answered Willy.

"I don't know," said Ace. "If those kids give me any trouble . . . *wham!*" He slammed his fist down hard. "They'll be sorry!"

It was only a few minutes later when Ace threw open the rear door of the van. Light streamed in, and Danny and Megan blinked their eyes. They were in a garage filled with other white trucks. Tools hung on the walls. Tires lined the floor.

Ace grabbed Megan by the arm. "Get out of there." He pulled her forward so fast she almost fell on her face.

"Don't you dare hurt her," Danny shouted. Even though his hands were tied, he jumped down and slammed his shoulder against Ace.

He fell over sideways. "I thought Willy shut you up," he snarled. "If you don't close your trap, I'll find a better way to do it."

"You don't scare me," Danny snapped back. "But you know, you could make a good living haunting houses."

Ace raised his arm and clenched his fist right under Megan's chin. "Keep quiet or she gets it."

Danny could tell that Ace was even more angry than before. He feared he might hurt Megan, so he didn't dare reply.

Ace then shoved them both against the wall. "Stay there and don't move. Don't even breathe." He turned to Willy and asked, "Do you really think the loot will be safe here?"

"Sure! No one knows where we are. Besides, they'll be looking for that other truck. Even if they do start searching the vans, I'll stack some of these tires in the back, so if anyone looks inside, they'll think it's full of them."

"Good plan," said Ace.

Willy shoved in the last tire that would fit and slammed the door. "Now get those two and follow me!" He led them over to a large metal grate on the wall and pried at the edge with a screwdriver. When it popped off, he said, "Ace, you go first." He motioned for Danny and Megan to follow.

After everyone was inside the dark tunnel, Willy climbed in and carefully replaced the grating. "Nobody will know we came this way." He ordered the trio to move forward into the black passageway. They stumbled through the darkness when, without warning, the lights went on!

"What the . . . ?" yelled Ace.

"It's just me," Willy explained, his hand on a light switch.

Megan turned around. "Where are we?"

Willy stared at her. He looked puzzled. "Wait a minute," he said. "I think I know you. You're the manager's daughter—Megan . . . Megan Kane. You're always nosing around the park."

"Yeah, I'm Megan Kane. And my father will tear this place apart until he finds us. He won't stop until I'm rescued. You might as well give yourself up right now."

Ace snickered. "Your father will never find us down here."

Megan glared at him. "Oh, yes, he will. You don't have enough brains to outsmart him."

"She's right," Danny added. "With a midget

mind like yours, I don't think you can count to twenty without taking your shoes off."

"Shut up," yelled Willy. "And keep moving."

Willy barked out orders, directing Ace through the winding, narrow passageway. They seemed to walk forever, moving up and down and around corridors that looked exactly alike. There were no doors or windows anywhere. Then all of a sudden, they passed in front of a door marked EXIT.

Megan nodded toward it so that only Danny could see her. She signaled for him to go through the door.

Danny shook his head, and Megan immediately let out a piercing scream. She stomped on Willy's foot and raced down the tunnel away from the door.

"Come back here," he shouted, limping after her.

Danny took his cue. He dove for the exit and kicked open the door.

Ace sped after him. "You're not getting away from me, you little punk!"

"Run, Danny, run," yelled Megan.

Ace leaped into the air and tackled Danny. They both fell to the ground.

When Megan looked back, Willy grabbed

her by the arm and pulled her around. "Oh, Danny, are you hurt?" she shouted.

Danny rubbed his neck. "I'm okay. But I sure wish that guy would sit on a firecracker and shoot himself into outer space."

"Face it, kid," said Ace, climbing to his feet. "You're just not tough enough for me!"

Danny stood up and looked him straight in the eye. "You know they named a town after you . . . Marblehead, Massachusetts."

Ace just sneered at him.

"You're not so tough," said Danny. "I know what happens to people like you, who think with their fists."

"They win, that's what!" bragged Ace. "You're just a loser!"

"A loser!" yelled Megan. "He's no loser, he's Da—"

Danny shook his head at her. She quickly realized her mistake. If she told Ace who Danny really was, things might become even worse than they already were.

"Come on, you two," growled Willy. "Get moving. It's not much farther to the hiding place. Once we're there, no one will find us."

Chapter

8

THOUSANDS OF PEOPLE had poured into the amusement park the moment it opened. The place was packed. The adults were just as excited as the kids. Everyone was laughing and cheering, having a great time.

But Jonathan, Jordan, Donnie, and Joe couldn't join in the fun. They had to find Danny, Megan, and the stolen equipment truck. Fortunately, no one recognized them in their costumes, even though Jonathan's wig kept falling off.

"Which way do we go?" asked Joe.

"There's a map over there," said Jonathan,

pointing to a large wooden sign. "I think we should start at one end of the park and carefully search every inch until we cover the whole place."

"There's only four of us," Donnie replied, raising his Viking sword over his head. "It would take us all week if we did that. We need a better plan of attack! I say we charge ahead and follow our instincts."

"Well, then, what are we waiting for?" asked Jordan. He immediately headed into the crowd, his silver suit of armor clanging and crashing with every step.

"Hey, Sir Lancelot, wait for us," yelled Donnie, rushing after him.

Joe waddled along in his penguin suit as fast as he could, while Jonathan struggled to keep his grass skirt from sliding down with every step.

The New Kids darted through the sea of people, searching for clues.

"Look over there," yelled Joe, flapping his wings out in front of him. "There go two guys in white suits."

"I'm already there," cried Donnie. He sprung into action and maneuvered through the crowd in no time at all.

When the two men saw Donnie thrashing his Viking sword overhead, they started to run.

"Come back here," he yelled, racing after them. The others were close behind.

The men ran even faster. They sped behind the Arabian desert race and then darted around a giant igloo, nearly knocking down a man in an Eskimo suit. The New Kids drew closer as the two men jumped over a fence and ran behind the Greek Parthenon Playhouse. They disappeared inside.

The four singers were out of breath when they reached the back entrance of the huge white building, shaped like an ancient Greek temple. An angry security guard, dressed as an astronaut, stopped them at the door. "Where do you think you're going?"

Donnie explained who he was. He told him he thought the two men might have been the ones who stole their equipment.

The guard laughed. "No way," he said. "That was Jeff and Kyle. They've been working on this ride since early this morning. They just went out for a five-minute break."

Jonathan's wig bobbed up and down as he let out a laugh. "Haawh! Haawh!" He then pointed around to the side of the temple. "Look! *All* the people who work here have on white costumes. They're wearing Greek togas on top of their white shirts and pants."

Donnie shrugged his shoulders. "Well, we tried, so let's get back out there and try some more. It's the New Kids to the rescue!"

"New Kids?" said a short blond girl who was walking nearby. "Are the New Kids here yet?"

"We were just wondering that ourselves," said Donnie, trying not to smile and give away his identity. "We're big fans of theirs!"

"Me, too," Joe added. "Awk! Awk!"

"I *love* the New Kids!" said the girl. "I came two hundred miles just to see them tonight."

"Who's your favorite one?" Jordan asked mischievously.

"Donnie!" she replied. "He's the greatest."

"What about Joe?" asked Joe, wiggling his penguin wings. "Don't you like him?"

"Oh, he's awfully cute, but not as cute as Donnie."

"What about Jordan?" Jordan asked. "Isn't he a great dancer?"

"Not as good as Donnie!"

Donnie stood up even straighter and nudged Jonathan's arm. Jonathan just laughed and shook his head.

The blond girl then inspected his blond wig

more closely. "You know, you kind of look like one of the New Kids yourself."

"No way," said Donnie, putting his arm around Jonathan's shoulder. "But people are always telling us that. Don't you think Bob here looks just like Jordan?"

The girl shook her head. "No," she said. "In fact, none of you look anything like them. I guess I want to see the New Kids so bad that everyone looks like them to me. Sorry."

"That's okay," said Jordan, taking her hand. He lowered his head, lifted the visor of his helmet, and gently kissed her fingers. "If I were a New Kid," he told her, "I'd want to meet a fair maiden like you."

The girl's eyes widened. "Really?"

Jonathan grabbed Jordan by the arm. "Hey, loverboy, we've got to get moving."

"Goodbye," Jordan yelled, as Jonathan pulled him back into the crowd.

While the four of them headed in one direction, Dick Scott was driving Rabbit through the park in the opposite direction. The pair rode in one of the white park maintenance vans, sitting up above the crowd, searching everything in sight, desperately looking for clues.

"I'm sorry I messed up," said Rabbit. "If I could have told you what was written on those white coveralls, maybe we wouldn't be in this mess."

"Don't be so hard on yourself," Dick replied. "You're one of the best sound men we've got, even if you can't read."

"So I'm not going to be fired?"

"Of course not, you're too valuable," said the manager, as he rounded the corner. "Maybe it's none of my business, Rabbit, but why didn't you ever learn to read?"

Rabbit hung his head down sadly. "Maybe it was because we moved around a lot. I went to at least fifteen different schools. I got so far behind I couldn't catch up. Then all of a sudden I was too embarrassed to admit that I didn't know how to read. From then on I did everything I could to hide it from people."

"That must have been hard work," said Dick.

"I'll say," Rabbit replied. "Some days I felt like I was trying to nail Jell-O to a tree."

Dick's warm fatherly smile spread across his face. "I understand. I'd like to help you learn to read if I can. I'm sure we can work something out."

"Thanks, Dick," said Rabbit. "Oh, look,

there's Phil. Maybe he's got some news. Hey, Phil, any luck?"

"Not yet," he replied. "Nobody's seen any sign of Danny, Megan, or the equipment truck anywhere."

Underneath the fury of activity in the park, Willy threw open a steel door at the end of a long narrow tunnel. "This is it," he said, directing everyone inside. The small room was filled from floor to ceiling with computer panels, each one covered with dials and switches. An empty table and two chairs sat in the middle of the room.

Ace pushed Danny through the doorway and dragged Megan right behind him. "You two sit on the floor over there, and don't even think of making a sound." He then pulled the ropes around Danny's wrists even tighter, just to let him know he meant it.

But Danny wasn't afraid of Ace. "I don't know what makes you tick," he said, "but I hope it's a time bomb."

Ace whipped around and shook his fist under his nose. "And this is about to go off in your face."

"Shut up, both of you," yelled Willy. He

then told Danny and Megan to sit down in front of one of the computer terminals.

"Hey, Willy, where are we?"

"This is the computer control room for the park's water system. Unless one of the water pipes breaks, nobody's going to come down here and find us."

"It sure gives me the creeps," Ace said. "I feel like I'm suffocating. What are we supposed to do all day? Maybe I'll listen to this walkie talkie." He switched it on but didn't hear a thing, so he angrily threw it in the corner of the room.

"Relax," said Willy. "I brought along a deck of cards. Maybe I can win some of that money we're going to make when we sell all the equipment."

Ace sat down at the table. He lit a cigarette, and Willy dealt out the cards. "You won't win any money off me if your plan doesn't work."

"It'll work," replied Willy. "Tonight we drive out of here, tomorrow we fence the stuff, and the day after that we're free."

"How much do you think it will bring?"

"Thirty grand," said Willy. "Some of that junk is real expensive."

Ace drew a card from the deck. "Thirty

thousand," he grumbled. "We should have kidnapped one of those New Kids. The ransom would bring us a million bucks! Then we'd be set for life. No more of this nickel-and-dime stuff."

"You're crazy," said Willy. "Kidnapping is too dangerous. I don't want to spend the rest of my life in a federal prison. Besides, those rock musicians have so many bodyguards we'd never get anywhere near them."

"Oh, no," Megan whispered to Danny. "What if they find out who you are?"

"Don't worry," he said quietly. "We'll get out of here before they do."

"How?" she asked. "This park is so big I don't think anyone will look down here for days."

Danny thought for a moment. Then he spoke even more quietly when he asked, "These computers control all the water in the park, right?"

"Yeah."

"If we turn off the water, someone will have to come fix it."

Megan shook her head. "But look at how many buttons and switches there are. We'll never be able to find the right one."

Danny inspected the control panel right

beside him. It was covered with round pressure gauges. As he looked at them more closely, he spotted a black metal lever labeled NIAGARA FALLS FOUNTAIN.

"What's that?" he asked, motioning to the lever.

"It's the big fountain in the center of the park."

"Hey," yelled Ace. "You two stop whispering."

"Aw, let 'em talk," Willy said. "They can't do anything. Leave 'em alone and play your card."

Danny leaned closer to Megan. "I've got an idea," he said. "I'm going to signal for help."

Chapter
9

THE SUN MOVED down across the sky as Jonathan, Joe, Donnie, and Jordan continued their search. It was already dinner time and they still hadn't found a clue. But they pressed on, digging through the crowd, climbing under the rides, and looking behind every single door they could open and even some they couldn't.

Jonathan became even more worried when he realized that time was slipping away. "We're not getting anywhere," he said. "All we're doing is going around in circles."

"You're right," Donnie replied. "We need a better plan. We won't have a concert tonight if we don't hurry up and find Danny and that musical equipment."

"What more can we do?" asked Joe.

"I don't know, but we've got to think of something pretty soon." Donnie climbed up on top of a trash container. He scanned over the huge bustling crowd. "They're in here somewhere, but where? There must be a million places to hide."

Jordan tipped back the visor of his armored helmet. "This costume is really getting hot. I'm burning up inside. I feel like a meatloaf that's been left in the oven too long."

"You smell like it, too," said Joe. "Phew!"

"No, really, I'm feeling kind of sick. I've got to get out of this thing." Jordan started to pull off the helmet.

"No, wait!" yelled Jonathan. "We'll be in even bigger trouble if someone sees who you really are."

"Look," said Joe, pointing over to the souvenir booth. "They sell hats and stuff. Maybe we can get something else for you to wear."

"I'll run over and see what I can find," Donnie exclaimed. He turned to leave, then stopped suddenly. "I don't have any money on me."

"Me, neither," said Jonathan.

Joe tried to feel his pants pockets through his bulky penguin suit. "I can't tell if I have any money."

"I do," said Jordan.

"But how are we going to get at it?" asked Donnie. "You'll have to take that armor off somewhere. But where?"

Jonathan frantically looked for a safe place. "Behind that control booth." He pointed to a little straw hut standing beside the African Safari water ride.

The four singers raced over behind it and immediately pulled off Jonathan's costume. All he had on underneath was a pair of high-top tennis shoes and his blue jeans.

"Give me your money," said Donnie.

When Jordan handed him the few dollars he had in his pocket, a security guard grabbed Donnie by the arm. "I caught you," declared an Asian man wearing a Scottish kilt. "You're coming with me. All of you."

"But . . . but . . . you don't understand," said Jonathan.

"Don't say another word," the guard angrily replied. "I know who you are."

"You do?" asked Joe, pulling off his penguin head.

"You're that gang of muggers that was reported to be robbing people in the park."

"No way," Donnie protested. "We're the New Kids on the Block."

"Well, I don't care if you're new at this game or you've been doing it for years. You're still coming with me."

Jordan stepped forward. "There's been a big misunderstanding here." He tried to explain, but the guard didn't believe him. "See those T-shirts for sale over at the souvenir booth? That's us."

The guard took one look at Jonathan, Jordan, Donnie, and Joe, then he examined the T-shirts more closely. "Hey, it really *is* you."

"That's right," said Jordan.

Jonathan nudged Donnie in the arm and pointed over to a group of girls nearby. "Those five girls are staring at us," he said. "I think they know who we are."

Before he could say another word, the girls shouted, "*It's them! The New Kids!*"

"Oh, no, we've got to get out of here!" cried Donnie.

The girls ran right toward them, and the New Kids turned and raced away. The screaming fans were right behind them.

Jordan was out in front. He could move faster than the others, because he had left his heavy suit of armor behind. Joe was struggling to bring up the rear. He gripped the penguin head under his arm, as he staggered and stumbled through the crowd.

Jonathan almost lost his blond wig when he slipped on a piece of cardboard and went flying forward. He caught his balance just in time, before he nearly crashed into a big fat man eating a giant ice cream cone.

The girls were screaming at the top of their lungs. Everyone turned to look. But the New Kids kept on running. When they sped around a corner, a white van pulled up beside them. "It's Rabbit!" yelled Donnie.

"Hop in," said the sound man.

Donnie and Jordan jumped into the side door, and Jonathan tumbled in after them.

"Awk! Awk!" cried Joe, running to catch up. "Don't leave me behind."

The screaming fans were right on his heels. "Joe! Joe!" they shouted. "Don't go!"

Joe reached for Jordan's outstretched hand. He grabbed ahold of it and sailed inside.

"Welcome aboard," said Donnie, slamming the van door shut. "Rabbit, get us out of here!"

Rabbit sped left, then right down a deserted side street, and, within seconds, the fans were out of sight.

"Whew!" said Joe, wiping his forehead. "That was close. I thought I was going to be a Kentucky Fried Penguin."

Donnie climbed up into the front passenger seat. "It's lucky you came along when you did. Any word on Danny, Megan, or the stolen equipment?"

Rabbit shook his head. "No, nothing yet. Dick went to give pictures of Danny to all of the security people. You know, he's really angry at you guys. Biscuit came and told him how you snuck off. He gave me orders to find you and bring you back."

"No, Rabbit, you can't," Donnie pleaded.

Joe leaned over the front seat. "Oh, please don't. We'll do anything if you'll let us stay out in the park and keep searching."

"Yeah," added Jordan. "I'll let you listen to all my jazz tapes."

Rabbit hesitated. But only for a moment. "Okay, I'll let you stay out, just don't tell Dick."

"No way," said Jonathan.

Rabbit then turned the van down another back alley. "I haven't searched this area yet."

"Drive slow," said Jonathan, "so we can keep a sharp eye out for clues."

Rabbit and the New Kids carefully inspected everything as they moved along an alley behind the rides. But they saw nothing.

When they circled back around to the center of the park, huge crowds of people blocked the road. Rabbit stopped the van and waited for them to move aside.

Jordan found a green maintenance shirt in the back and put it on to cover his bare chest. He was watching out the open window when suddenly he yelled out, "Hey, everybody, look over there!"

"What is it?" asked Jonathan. "Do you see Danny?"

"No, but there's something strange about that fountain."

"What?" asked Joe. "It just looks like a model of Niagara Falls to me."

Jordan stared at the falling water and tapped his hand against his leg. "The water in that fountain is spurting out to the beat of a song."

"Plenty of fountains move in time to music," said Donnie. "They call them dancing fountains."

"But do they spurt water in time to one of *our* songs?" asked Jordan.

"Song?" asked Joe. "What song? All I hear is Reggae music coming from that Jamaican Hurricane ride over there."

"It's 'Hangin' Tough,'" said Jordan. "That fountain is moving to the beat of 'Hangin' Tough'!"

"He's right," said Rabbit. "If you listen carefully, you can hear the water splashing in time with the song."

"Maybe you can," said Joe. "But you've got superhuman ears!"

Donnie followed the rhythm as the fountain's waters rose and fell. "Yeah, that's our song."

*Listen up everybody, if you want to take a
    chance,
Just get on with it boy, and do the New
    Kid's dance.*

"Do you suppose the park did that specially for us?" asked Joe.

"I don't think so," said Jordan. "If they did, then they would have played our music along with it."

"Why would anyone want to make the fountain dance to one of our songs?" asked Joe.

"Maybe it's some kind of signal!" Donnie answered.

"Yeah," exclaimed Jordan. "Maybe it's Danny. I'll bet he's trying to send us some kind of message."

"What should we do now?" asked Joe.

"Why don't we find out where this fountain is being controlled from?" said Jonathan. "If we go there, we might discover a clue. We might even find Danny!"

Donnie stuck his head out the window and searched the area. "I don't see a door around here."

"The controls could be anywhere," said Jordan. "My guess is that they're under the park. We need to find somebody who can take us there."

Rabbit pointed into the crowd. "There's a security guard over there." He then swiftly drove the van up beside him. The guard was wearing a London policeman uniform. His red name tag said BERT. Donnie leaned out the window and told him who they were. He then explained about the fountain. Bert immediately switched on his walkie talkie and notified security to search the tunnels. After that, he called the maintenance department. There was a short pause before the directions to the control room sounded out from the tiny speaker. "We can get inside the tunnels through there," Bert said, pointing to a door on the side of a Dutch windmill.

"We've got to move fast," Jordan replied. "The water in the fountain has stopped moving up and down."

Rabbit pulled the van over to the windmill. Bert unlocked the wooden door and threw it open. He led everyone down into a narrow passageway. The tunnel twisted right, then left, and around a dozen corners. "We should be almost there," he said.

When they spotted a doorway up ahead, Bert held up his hand for everyone to stop. "That's it," he whispered. "I'll go in first. You guys stay back. The thieves might have a gun." Bert inched over and silently slipped his key into the lock. He turned it without making a sound.

He then kicked the door open and charged inside!

But when he flicked on the lights, no one was there!

The room was empty.

"Are you sure this is the right place?" asked Donnie, rushing in behind him.

"This is it," answered Bert. "Look, the lever that controls the fountain is over there."

"Somebody was just here," said Jonathan. "That cigarette is still burning. Whoever it was cleared out in a hurry."

"Megan was here!" yelled Joe.

"How can you tell?" asked Donnie.

"There's a heart scratched into the concrete floor. It says M.K. plus D.W. Megan Kane plus Danny Wood!"

Jonathan looked worried. "But we don't know if Danny was here, too!"

"Yes, we do," Joe replied confidently. "Look at these little black marks. Danny always rubs his heels on the floor whenever he's bored. His black shoes make scuff marks just like this."

"Okay," said Jonathan. "So Danny was here. *But where is he now?*"

"Hey, look what I found," cried Jordan. He held up a long, slim walkie talkie and pushed a button on the side.

"They'll never find us here," said a voice through the speaker. *"After dark we can sneak out and get the loot."*

Then a familiar voice sounded: *"You dirtbags won't get away with this!"*

"Danny!" cried the New Kids.

Donnie grabbed Bert by the arm. "Can you trace that radio signal?"

Bert shook his head. "There are too many radios like this in the park. Nearly every employee has one."

"Maybe the thieves are park employees," Jordan suggested.

"Quiet, you guys," said Jonathan. "They're saying something else."

"My father and his security guards are going to find us any minute."

"That's Megan!" Joe shouted.

All of a sudden, Megan screamed.

FZZZZT!

The radio went dead.

"What happened?" yelled Donnie. "Jordan, press the button again."

He tried and tried, but the signal wouldn't come back. "It's no use. I can't get it to work."

Joe kicked the table. "That was our only clue. Now we may never find them in time!"

"I think I know where they are," said Rabbit.

"Where?" asked Donnie.

"Just before the walkie talkie went dead, I heard the sound of a roller-coaster drive chain in the background."

Joe jumped into the air and cheered. "Those ears of yours are worth a million dollars."

"But there are at least six roller coasters in the park," said Jonathan.

"It's the Mount Everest," Rabbit replied. "I'm certain of it. I drove by it earlier. I may not remember faces, but I never forget a sound."

"The Mount Everest," said Jonathan. "That's the biggest one in the park, isn't it?"

"Right," Bert answered, as he activated his radio. He relayed the news to the security forces.

"Which way to Mount Everest?" Donnie asked.

"Follow me," ordered Bert. "We can be there in five minutes."

Everyone raced for the door.

"You're amazing," Joe said to Rabbit. "You really have superhuman ears. We should get them gold-plated!"

Chapter
10

WHEN DANNY SHOVED Willy to the ground, his walkie talkie smashed against the cement and broke apart. Megan then kicked Ace in the stomach as hard as she could, and he doubled over in agony. Megan and Danny both bolted out the door, Danny slammed it behind him, and they took off running.

"We've got to get out of here," Danny said, pulling at the rope around his hands. It didn't budge. "Do you know where we are?"

"I'm . . . I'm not sure," answered Megan. "After they moved us from the Niagara Falls

. . . they took us up . . . we must be underneath one of the big rides, but I don't know which one."

"We'll find our way out," he said, running as fast as he could. Megan struggled to keep up, as they turned corner after corner.

"I don't see an exit anywhere," said Danny. "I think we're going around in circles."

"You are!" yelled Ace, leaping out in front of them. "You're circling around inside the Mount Everest roller coaster." He shook a long metal wrench right in Danny's face. "Now march back down the tunnel."

"Where are you taking us?"

"Back where we came from," said Willy, shoving him forward.

When they returned, Ace grabbed Danny by the collar and snarled, "If you two try anything else, we may never let you out of here." Ace stopped suddenly. He glanced down at one of the advertising posters lying on the table and then looked back at Danny. "Hey, wait a minute. What's your name, kid?"

"Danny."

"Danny what?"

"Danny Kowalski."

"Show me your wallet, Danny Kowalski."

"What for?"

Ace waved the wrench under Danny's nose. "Because I say so. Just do it."

"I don't have it with me."

"Then what's this?" he asked, tapping Danny's back pocket with the wrench.

"Solid muscle?"

Ace yanked out the wallet. "It says here you're Daniel William Wood from Dorchester, Massachusetts."

Willy grabbed it away from him. "Danny Wood! Danny Wood . . . of the New Kids on the Block."

"The New Kids?" asked Danny. "What's that?"

"Quit fooling around," said Willy. "You're one of the members of that rock band."

Ace whistled in amazement. "You mean instead of just stealing their instruments, we've stolen one of *them?*"

"That's right," said Willy. "But now this changes everything. There are probably a million cops crawling all over this place. I wonder what we should do now?"

"You could let us go," said Megan.

"I've got a better idea," Ace replied. "How about we hold Danny for ransom? He ought to be worth a million dollars."

"I don't know," Willy said doubtfully. "We

could get ourselves into real trouble if we pull something like that."

"We might as well try it," said Ace. "Everyone probably thinks they've been kidnapped anyway."

"Maybe you're right."

"You'll never get away with it," yelled Megan.

Ace just laughed at her. "Maybe we should ransom you, too. Your dad ought to have some dough stashed away. If not, the park will probably pay to get you back."

"One thing at a time," said Willy. "We've got to figure out how to get those two out of here as soon as possible. They'll be tearing this place apart until they find them. Our only chance is to get as far away as fast as we can."

Before he could say another word, the door burst open.

Donnie rushed in. The others were right behind him.

Willy leaped to his feet, and Ace threw a chair across the room. It smashed into Jonathan and pushed him over on top of Jordan and Joe.

Willy swung at Rabbit, but he ducked down just in time. Rabbit made a grab for Willy, when, all of a sudden, the lights went out.

Megan shouted at the top of her lungs, "Don't let those creeps get out the door!"

"Where's the light switch?" yelled Joe.

"Where's the door?" cried Donnie.

"Wait a minute," said Jonathan, switching back on the light. "Where are the crooks?"

"They took off," said Bert.

"Well, they won't get far," declared Donnie. "Let's go get 'em."

Jonathan swiftly untied Megan and Danny, and they raced out after him.

Willy and Ace sped through the tunnel as fast as they could.

"We'll get back to the van," said Willy, "and then we'll make a break for it."

"Which way do we go?" asked Ace.

"There's a ladder just up ahead. It leads outside to the top of the roller coaster. We can climb down from there."

Ace shuddered. "Ah . . . this isn't the best time to tell you this, but . . . ah . . . I'm afraid of heights."

Willy shook his head, then he sped around the corner and pointed to a ladder up ahead. "There it is. It's our only chance. Either climb up it or go back and turn yourself in."

"That's not much of a choice," Ace said.

"I'll try to climb it, but if I fall, give me a nice funeral."

"Here we go," said Willy. He grabbed on to the iron rungs of the ladder.

As soon as they disappeared into the dark narrow passageway, Jordan flew around the corner. "I was sure they went down here."

"What about that ladder over there on the wall?" said Jonathan. "Maybe they went up there."

"I think it leads outside," said Bert.

Rabbit ran over and looked up the tunnel. It was too dark to see anything. He pressed his ear against the metal rungs. "There's someone up there. I hear them."

Danny immediately scrambled up the ladder after them. Everyone else piled on right behind him.

Up ahead, Willy could feel the ladder start to vibrate. "They're following us."

"I think I'm going to be sick," said Ace.

"Hang on, we're almost there. The exit is up here somewhere." He reached the end of the ladder and fumbled around in the dark, searching for the hatch. "Ah, here it is."

He threw it open and climbed out onto the

top of the Mount Everest roller coaster. The park spread out below in every direction.

Ace pulled himself onto the white cement surface, painted to look like snow. "How do we get down?"

Willy pointed to the roller-coaster track running right beside them. "The cars will be coming by here any minute. When they move slower to go over the top, we'll jump inside. Here they come now!"

Ace cautiously peered over the edge of the giant mountain. A row of cars had just looped upside down and was heading straight at them. "I'm getting in that?" he asked nervously.

"If you don't," said Willy, "it's a long climb down."

"Or a long fall."

Willy leaned closer to the track. "They're almost here. Get ready to jump."

Just as the cars shot up to the top, Danny popped out of the hatch. Ace and Willy leaped into the empty front seat of a roller-coaster car before he could reach them. A woman in one of the back cars let out a scream. No one heard her over the roaring sounds of the roller coaster.

The cars started downward, and Danny ran

after them. He jumped into the air and grabbed for the last one. He caught it. The roller coaster picked up speed. Danny pulled himself inside, just before it spun upside down.

When the coaster reached the bottom of the ride, it slowed down just enough so Danny could climb out onto the side. He moved hand over hand along the outside railing of the cars, inching closer to Ace and Willy.

"Young man, will you get back in your seat?" an old woman said angrily.

"Grandma!" shouted the young girl sitting beside her. "That's Danny Wood of the New Kids on the Block!"

When she said that, Ace jumped up, turned around, and took a swing at Danny.

"Can I have your autograph?" yelled the girl. "I just love your records."

"Maybe later," Danny struggled to answer. "I'm a little tied up right now."

All of a sudden the roller coaster zoomed up and to the right. It slid through a tight curve and started to loop.

"We're going upside down," warned the girl. "Hang on, Danny!"

"I will," he yelled, as he gripped the railing with all his strength.

The coaster dove back around, and Willy shouted, "Ace! Jump off here!"

The car slowed again and Willy dove out. Ace hesitated, but he jumped out after him.

Danny pulled two tickets from his shirt pocket and threw them to the girl. "These are for tonight's show," he said. "Bring your grandmother. She might like it."

The girl scooped up the tickets and held them tight. "I'll be there," she yelled as Danny leaped off the car, tearing after Ace and Willy.

The grandmother smiled. "Such a handsome young man. Does he sing well?"

"Oh, Grandma! Does he!"

Chapter

11

ANOTHER STRING OF roller-coaster cars raced to the bottom. When it slowed down, Jonathan, Jordan, Donnie, Joe, Megan, Rabbit, and Bert jumped out.

"Can anyone see where Danny went?" asked Joe, putting back on his penguin head.

"No!" said Donnie.

Jordan ducked down behind him so no one would recognize him. He then pointed to the right. "Hey, look over there," he said. "See that screaming crowd of girls?"

"Uh-oh," cried Donnie. "I bet they're running after Danny."

"How are we going to catch up to him?" exclaimed Jonathan. "If those girls see us, they'll be all over us, too. Then we'll never reach him."

"And he's getting farther and farther away every second," said Jordan.

Donnie leaned back his head while he tried to figure out what to do. "I've got it!" he shouted. "Let's go *over* them."

"How?" asked Jonathan.

"We can take the tramway," he said, pointing to the small yellow cars hanging overhead. "We'll track them from up there."

Bert held up his walkie talkie. "I can radio their position to the other security guards."

Everyone but Megan scrambled over to the Swiss Skyway ride. She took off after Danny.

The Skyway's round cars were shaped like wheels of cheese. There was a big, long line out front.

"We work here," said Donnie, running past the attendant and through the gate.

"Yeah," Jonathan added. "We wouldn't be caught dead in these silly costumes if they weren't paying us."

Joe waddled after them in his penguin suit. Jordan hid between Bert and Rabbit, as they followed them through.

The attendant, wearing leather shorts and a green felt hat, winked to them. "I know how you feel." He directed Jonathan, Jordan, and Joe to the first skycar. Donnie, Rabbit, and Bert climbed into the second one. The car quickly rose into the air and over the park.

"I think I see Danny," Jonathan yelled back to the others.

"Yeah, that's him all right," said Donnie. "Look at him run!"

"There goes those other two guys," shouted Joe. "The ones who stole our stuff. They're right in front of him."

"I'll radio their positions," Bert said, as he pressed the power button. Nothing happened. He pressed it again. "Oh, no!"

"What's wrong?" asked Donnie.

Bert shook the walkie talkie. "I can't get this thing to work."

"If we don't radio for help, they might get away," said Rabbit.

"No they won't," Donnie replied. "Not if I can do anything about it." He quickly scanned out over the park. Then he yelled up to Jonathan, Jordan, and Joe: "Hey, you guys, get ready to jump!"

"Are you totally wacked?" yelled Jonathan.

"Just trust me. See that giant trampoline up ahead? It's as big as a football field and completely empty. When we pass over it, jump out on top of it. Okay?"

Jonathan shook his head.

"We have to," Donnie insisted. "It's getting later every minute. If we don't do something right away, we'll miss the concert."

"Okay," Jonathan replied.

"Here it comes," yelled Donnie. "Everybody get ready."

When the yellow skycars swung over the huge trampoline, Donnie climbed onto the edge of the skycar. "Here goes!" he yelled, as he plunged off the side. He safely landed in the middle and bounced back up into the air. Everyone else jumped down beside him.

"Hey, this is great!" said Joe, flipping over backwards.

Jonathan stood up and yelled, "Those two guys just ran into that Aztec video arcade."

"Get 'em!" cried Donnie.

Ace nervously glanced over his shoulder. "Do you see that Danny kid anywhere?"

Willy shook his head. "Nope. I think that crowd of girls will keep him busy for a while.

That was a smart idea of yours, pointing to him and shouting, 'There's one of the New Kids.'"

"Yeah." Ace laughed. "They were all over him in two seconds. I can't wait . . ."

But before he could say another word, Jordan leaped out in front of him.

Willy spun around and came face to face with Joe. He grabbed the singer by the shoulders and threw him into a video-game machine. "Run for it," Willy yelled to Ace.

Rabbit and Jordan tried to stop Ace, but he easily broke away and dove for the exit. Willy scrambled past Donnie by jumping up onto a pinball machine. He ran across the glass tops of the entire row.

Everyone jumped back out of his way. They started screaming and running in every direction, making it impossible for the New Kids to reach Ace and Willy before they escaped outside.

Donnie was the first to break out. "There they are," he said, pointing to the Armenian Merry-Go-Round."

"We can catch them," exclaimed Joe.

They all took off after Willy and Ace, darting in and out of the crowd, over and under rides, and smashing through a concession stand, spilling chili and corn bread every-where.

They charged on.

Willy and Ace were pulling even farther ahead, when, all of a sudden, they leaped over a fence.

"Grab one of these go-carts," said Willy. "Head for the garage where we hid the van. We'll bust through the back gate and make a run for it."

"Right," Ace replied. He slid into the tiny green vehicle and sped down the miniature *Grand Prix* track.

"They're getting away!" yelled Joe, when he reached the fence.

"Daredevil Donnie's going to show you how to drive like the wind." He jumped into a red go-cart and took off.

Everyone else grabbed one and raced after him.

Danny had lost sight of Willy and Ace when the swarm of fans closed in around him. He tried to run but they grabbed at him no matter which way he turned.

RRRRIP!

"Hey, not my shirt!" he pleaded.

He held on tight to what was left of it when a

horn blasted through the crowd. "Get out of the way," yelled Megan. She drove a park utility cart up beside him. "Hop on, Danny!"

He jumped inside, and Megan sped away as fast as she could.

"That was close," said Danny, wiping his forehead.

"Are you okay?" she asked. "Oh, look at your shirt, there's nothing left of it."

"I'm all right, thanks to you," he said, gratefully patting her on the shoulder. "Where are we going?"

Megan sped around a corner. "To go get all of your instruments and equipment. There's just enough time if we hurry."

Danny hung on to the dashboard, as they raced toward the garage where the van was hidden.

"There's Willy and Ace," yelled Danny, pointing to the two go-carts up ahead.

"And here come the New Kids, right behind us," said Megan. She pushed the accelerator to the floor and charged right at Willy.

He spotted her coming. "That kid is insane," he yelled. "She's going to ram us!"

"Not me!" Ace shouted. He spun the wheel and skidded to the right. Megan rushed up behind him, but he slid around the corner before she could reach him. Ace pulled ahead, Megan pumped the gas, and her vehicle lunged forward.

Danny stood up as they went speeding closer. With a burst of speed, he leaped onto the back of Ace's go-cart. One arm went around Ace's neck and the other reached down and turned off the ignition.

The cart rolled to a stop. "Let go of me!" he howled.

But Danny held him tight in a headlock. "You know, Ace, you're the kind of guy who goes through life pushing doors marked *pull*. Well, you won't be doing much of either for a *long* time."

Bert and five security guards ran over and took Ace into custody.

"Where's Willy?" Danny asked Megan when she drove up beside him.

"There he is!" she said. "Donnie's going after him, and the others are closing in behind him."

"Give yourself up!" Donnie yelled.

"Never!" Willy shouted back, as Jordan raced along his left.

"You can't mess with the New Kids and get away with it!" he cried.

"We'll see about that!" snarled Willy. He

jerked to the side and tried to bump Jordan out of the way, but Jordan held steady. Then he tried to cut past Donnie, but Donnie drew closer. Willy pushed the pedal to the floor. The Niagara Falls Fountain was dead ahead. "If I can just get past these guys and—"

SPLASH!

Willy plunged right into the water as Donnie and Jordan swerved to each side. The others screeched to a halt just in time.

Within seconds, a dozen guards surrounded the fountain and handcuffed Willy. He was kicking and screaming as they dragged him away.

"Now all we have to do is find our equipment," said Jonathan.

Megan and Danny pulled up next to him. "I know where it is," she said. "Follow me." Driving like mad, she quickly led them to a maintenance building at the rear of the park.

Everybody piled inside. The van was still there. They were all relieved that the equipment hadn't been touched.

Donnie glanced at his watch. "We've got just enough time to get to the concert if we move fast." He hopped into the driver's seat. Jonathan and Joe climbed in beside him. The rest followed in Megan's cart. They darted and dodged through the crowd all the way back to the theater.

When they finally got there, Dick Scott ran outside, frantically waving his arms. "I'm glad you guys are all right. Hurry into the dressing room and get ready for the show. The roadies will get this stuff set up. Move fast, because the theater's already full and the crowd is getting anxious."

Megan showed her backstage pass and ran into the concert hall. She peeked out through the curtain. "The place is packed," she said to Biscuit, standing beside her. Everyone was whistling and clapping, cheering for the New Kids.

"It's always like this before the show," he explained. "The fans go wild."

In the dressing room, Danny climbed past Joe to grab his black shirt. Donnie and Jordan both crowded into the mirror to shave as quickly as possible, while Jonathan frantically searched for his other shoe.

"Where's Einstein?" asked Joe, still struggling out of his penguin suit.

"I'm over here," said the tutor. "What do you need?"

Joe finally yanked off the bulky costume and whispered in the tutor's ear. Einstein nodded. "I'd be glad to."

The New Kids scrambled to get dressed as the road crew set up the equipment faster than ever before. Dick was relieved when Rabbit told him that nothing was missing.

The crowd clapped louder and louder, yelling for Donnie, Danny, Jonathan, Jordan, and Joe.

When Jonathan finally found his shoe, they ran to the wing of the stage. They gathered together in a huddle as they did before every concert.

After a brief private moment together, Donnie yelled, "Let's go!"

"It's showtime," said Dick. "New Kids, do your thing!"

All five raced out in front of the crowd. They leaped into the air and spun around. The audience went wild, yelling and screaming and jumping to their feet. The noise didn't die down until Jordan began singing their first song.

Dick Scott breathed a sigh of relief. "They made it with one minute to spare. Those guys are the hardest working kids in show business."

"Rabbit," said Einstein, putting his arm on the sound man's shoulder. "Why don't we start our first reading lesson?"

"That would be great," he replied, with a big happy smile.

Megan could barely breathe, as she stood watching from the side of the stage. She couldn't believe she was actually there. It was like a dream come true.

The first song ended, and Danny grabbed the microphone. "We'd like to dedicate this next song to a very special friend of ours. If it hadn't been for her, we might not have made it to the concert tonight."

The spotlight flashed to the side of the stage.

"Everybody give a big hand to Megan Kane," he said, motioning for her to step forward.

The audience cheered.

Megan nearly fainted when Danny took her by the hand and pulled her onstage. He looked deep into her eyes, as he began to sing.

She knew she would remember every note for the rest of her life.

If you know anyone who has problems with reading and would like to help them, contact your local library or any of the following organizations:

Laubach Literacy Action
Box 131
Syracuse, NY 13210

Literacy Volunteers of America
5795 Widewaters Pkwy.
Syracuse, NY 13214

Reading Is Fundamental
600 Maryland Ave., S.W.
Suite 500
Washington, DC 20560

To find a local program for help with reading problems, call the national literacy hotline at 1-800-228-8813.